October 4, 1976

D0251281

B

S

THE MIRACLE SEASON

THE
MIRACLE
SEASON
Linda Cline

Berkley Publishing Corp.,
Distributed by
G. P. Putnam's Sons,
New York

SBN: 399-11654-0

Library of Congress Cataloging in Publication Data:
Cline, Linda.
The miracle season.

I. Title.
PZ4.C63944Mi [PS3553.L55] 813'.5'4 76-18070

PRINTED IN THE UNITED STATES OF AMERICA

THE MIRACLE SEASON

To Grandmama MAMIE HAY WHITEBURST, who raised me as her own, imparting values and strength upon which I draw to this day. She loved and spoiled me, and I shall cherish that forever.

FOREWORD

Fifteen years of study and constant association with animals has left me with the unsubstantiated but haunting conviction that, in certain unique instances, they can communicate on a plane equal to or surpassing humans.

The Intelligence Quotient of 180 or higher occurs in humans at the rate of about six in one million. If the mathematical probability is the same in creatures other than man, there are a thousand such animal geniuses born among vertebrates per generation. And if this is so, the miracle comes and goes and man never knows.

Who dares to deny that genius occurs in creatures other than man?

L.C.

PART ONE

Days of the Golden Miracle

I

A breeze too gentle to feel gave breath to sighing pines. The old crow teetered on the absolute apex of the tallest loblolly, wiping shreds of breakfast corn from his beak. He counter-balanced himself on his uncertain perch with body movements so subtle as to escape detection. His silhouette was as steady as deadwood. Tail-bobbers were young inexperienced birds. Crow Mayor was far too expert to waggle. His eyes, although dulled by time, were still keener than many and more alert than most. At a glance, he took in the raisin-flecks of fellow crows feeding in the field below.

There was a stately air to the old bird. His plumage no longer reflected sun rays from a sheen of blue-black; his feathers were losing their luster. The ten primary quills of the wings were tattered at the tips, and he had a balding spot midway between his tail and shoulders. Nonetheless, he had regal bearing. To forty rookeries he was known as "Crow Mayor." The title was a Spanish word.

To fledglings he would say in his melodic accent, "One does not say *may*-uhr. One says may-*ohr*."

3

Mayor meant "elder." It also meant greater, greatest, larger, older, senior, main, principal, and chief. Crow Mayor was all of these. Further, he was, as he would tell you, "a prophet."

"I am," Crow Mayor would state, "the son of a son of a son of a prophet and the longest-lived crow known to the councils of this continent."

It was a distinction merely to have remained alive for so many years. For that alone he would have earned the respect and awe of his tribe. However, the veneration he enjoyed was for more than just his age. Crow Mayor prophesied the Coming.

This event could not be far away. Because Crow Mayor realized he would soon die.

He could feel it. It was like flying without alighting for days. It was like being buffeted by thermal currents and pelted by driving rain. Like battling a headwind in the dead of winter with an empty craw, the stones grinding one another for lack of grain. At last, with exhaustion in every fiber of his body, sleep became the most important thing in the world. He ached for a warm nest and the comforting down of a mother long gone. He dreamed of solitude, tranquillity, and slumber. When at last he did sleep, he would awaken to find himself almost as exhausted as when first he closed his eyes. By this, he knew it wasn't far away. He was going to die.

Upon hearing this, young birds ruffled their feathers and shivered off prickling sensations. The young bird fears dying. He does not understand—and Crow Mayor had ceased trying to explain—why, to a very old bird, the thought of death's nest and eternal down becomes very appealing.

All birds can foretell the coming of a storm. The air pressure drops and their hollow bones expand, making them vaguely restless. They fly up, alight, lift off again, for no apparent reason. It's their hollow bones enlarging that causes it, as the air pressure within them equalizes to that without. For Crow Mayor, such daily barometric changes brought hours of aching joints.

His feet did not lock so automatically when he perched these days. In times past, as with younger birds, his feet would clamp three toes front and one to the back so tightly that no gale could blow him from his roost. Thus a bird may sleep without fear of falling in the night. Nowadays, though, Crow Mayor found himself subjected to the most ridiculous of happenstances. Several times he had awakened to find the community gathered silently about, looking at him in a peculiar manner. He was upside down! During the night he had slipped right over.

The first time it happened he had attempted to fly and cracked his head on a hardwood bole before he realized that up was down and down was the way he was trying to fly! Several yearlings had thereafter tried to duplicate the feat, thinking it some form of exercise that would bathe the brain with wisdom. Crow Mayor kept a tight beak and allowed them to think so. However, he was careful to clamp his feet a bit more securely these nights. When no one was looking he often provided himself a leaning post to insure his position.

By his aching bones, fading feathers, and weak clamp, Crow Mayor knew he would not live much longer. This did not make him unhappy. In fact, he became very excited because he knew that at last the Coming was near. Unless, of course, his father's prophecy was wrong—but Crow Mayor refused to consider such a possibility. One does not live one's life based on a lie. It had to be true.

"Before your existence is over," his papa had always said, "you will witness the Coming of Crow Corvus. Know him by the sign that marked you: a white-tipped feather in the crown. There will be other signs which I do not know, but which you will recognize when you see them. To Crow Corvus you must pass all the knowledge you have gained. You must protect and guide him. He is the only hope for the survival of crowdom. If he fails, the world as we know it will vanish."

"Will Crow Corvus succeed, Papa?"

The ancient seer would get a distant look in his ebony eyes. With a croaking voice he admitted: "That I do not know."

Over the years, Crow Mayor often doubted Papa's prophecy; often his faith would wane. But like the tail of a lizard, faith can be snapped off and it will regenerate itself. Now, having watched for signs all these years and aware that he would soon die, Crow Mayor was positive that this would be the season.

He wiped his beak on either side of a twig, cleaning it with passerine pleasure. He stared across the field at a distant farmhouse and detected a fearsome flicker of sun on steel. He looked toward an outpost where the community sentry was stationed, waiting. Did he not see? Crow Mayor resisted the urge to take wing, biding his time, still watching the sentry nearest the farm dwelling. In a moment the sharp "Cawt! Cawt!" came to his ears, and Mayor slipped off the tip of the pine, gliding. Proudly he noted to himself that he had been twice the distance from the rifle as the sentry was, and still he had seen it before the alert younger bird. Age and experience had their value.

The crows flew close to the treetops to avoid exposing themselves. Peaceful grazing in the cornfield was gone for this day. Crow Mayor skirted an oak where several birds had gathered out of curiosity, watching the escape route to see if anyone was caught.

Crow Mayor involuntarily darted in his flight as the explosive report of a shotgun reached his ears. A few doubting or negligent yearlings were getting a lesson about heeding the sentries! You could tell them a thousand times and it was as useless as telling a sparrow with mites not to scratch. Youth had to learn for itself. It was a cardinal rule.

Crow Mayor referred to the basic truths of life as "cardinal rules." He had learned human language in an amazing way, and he liked its precise terminology. It baffled and exasperated him, though, that the same humans who had made this splendid phrase had also given the word to a particularly odious sort of bird. "Any creature related to sparrows is incapable of deducing truths!" Crow Mayor declared.

He did not pretend to be free of prejudice. After all, sparrows had hounded crows for centuries. Flitting in to strike, the darting sparrows would always aim for the most tender quills, plucking them as a beleaguered crow lumbered away. Such birds as cardinals, buntings, and sparrows were enemies to crows. Mayor would never say something that gave these pests an iota of prestige.

Crow Mayor would say, a "cardinal rule" is a fundamental, not open to argument. For example, it was a cardinal rule that a farmer would not see a crow eating three times its body weight in insects each week; all the farmer saw was the crow collecting its wages in corn. Another cardinal rule was "Never share a tree with a possum." That dull-witted individual would as soon eat you in your sleep as not! He was not to be trusted no matter how he grinned as he waddled past. There was a cardinal rule about owls, which Crow Mayor called *sin*—another Spanish word meaning "without." Every rookery had sins watching it. Woe be to the crow when a sin found him out.

But cardinal rules certainly had nothing to do with cardinals.

Crow Mayor was very good at gliding. He had long ago mastered the art of lounging in flight over columns of rising warm air, lifting no more than an occasional feather to hold to his pattern. Now, slipping quietly through the woodland, he flapped his wings only as often as needed to stay at treetop level. Thus he avoided the keen eye of a hawk perched atop a distant dead tree. He also passed directly over two men hunting squirrel, and they never knew he was there.

He followed a familiar path, adjusting his flight at certain landmarks. He spied a sparrow carrying twigs in her beak and made a mental note to check the area more closely a few weeks later. There would be fresh eggs for breakfast one morning, if he were lucky.

He dropped his feet, spread his tail, and with a final flap or two of his wings, settled on an exposed limb over a stream of water. He took plenty of time to study the surrounding trees, shrubs, and vines. Long beyond the time most crows would have been satisfied, Mayor still watched, alert to danger, moving only his head in quick, jerking motions.

He saw a doe step gingerly from the underbrush, walking as deer do, on tiptoes. Her liquid brown eyes wide, cupped ears turning, she looked and listened for trouble. Her fear in this area was man, so she soon relaxed, spreading her forelegs and putting down her head to take long draughts from the clear creek.

It was only after Mayor had painstakingly examined every foot of the scene that he slipped off the limb and glided to the bank of the rivulet. Walking with stiff steps, shifting his weight from foot to foot, moving much as his ancestors the dinosaurs had moved, Crow Mayor approached the stream. A particularly enticing pebble caught his eye and he grabbed it up and swallowed. His craw had felt light the past few days and the added weight made him contented. The pebble was necessary, of course. Without it, food would lie in his craw unpulverized. He would soon be stuffed with whole kernels of corn and no way to get it ground, if he did not swallow an occasional stone to gnash the food particles to pieces.

Great grubs! A crawdad! Down it went. He had a special fondness for foods of the water. He had often wondered if perhaps a bit of the fish crow might not have slipped into his lineage somewhere along the way. Papa had always denied that.

He scooped water, threw back his head, and let it trickle down his throat. He repeated the action until his thirst was sated. Then, idly, he strolled along looking for interesting objects and fantasizing that he might find another crawdad. He did not. It's a lucky bird that discovers two crustaceans in a single lighting. Nonetheless, he searched for a while before returning to his limb to preen his feathers, taking oil from the nub atop his tail (and it was nearly dry) to apply to his coat.

His grooming completed, he was ready to take flight. He planned an excursion to a recently planted peanut patch—but something urged him to stay. He had long ago learned to obey these impulses and seldom regretted it. Once more alert, he scanned the creek banks and saw nothing amiss. He rose from limb to limb, extending his field of vision with each ascension. Carefully, still unsure of what he sought, he continued to seek. Finally, he saw it.

On a sandy knoll beneath a blackberry thicket, a rattlesnake was stalking a rabbit. Crow knew the rattler was female by her swollen sides and tapered tail. He watched frozen, almost hypnotized by the drama unfolding below.

The rabbit, accustomed to peril in the form of movement, looked right over the rattlesnake. His nose quivering, ears up, the rabbit's eyes were trained to a certain shape that to him meant danger. He did not notice the minute flicker of the rattler's black tongue. The checkered scalation of the reptile concealed her on the shadow-patterned pine needles beneath the tangled thicket. The snake knew that a movement would send the rabbit fleeing. The rattler used only her ventral muscles, lifting and moving forward beneath her body like the legs of a centipede. Crow Mayor took note of the silence that befell the area.

Except for the darting tongue, which the snake used to pick up the rabbit's scent, there was no telltale movement. When the rabbit looked up, alert, his jaws halting in mid-chew, the rattler paused and waited. Only when the rabbit's head went down to eat again did the rattler resume its stalking.

Tension mounted in the observers. One would have thought the rabbit would notice, but he did not. Then a strange thing happened. Crow Mayor had seen it occur many times before. The rabbit lifted his head, rising on his haunches, chewing. He wiped his nose once or twice with his forepaws, cleaning himself. Suddenly he saw the rattlesnake.

Did he flee those venomous fangs? Did he bound aside to safety? No. He froze like a furry stone, watching the reptile inching forward. The snake began to bend, her body pulling into a coil, looping like an S. The rabbit stopped chewing, one ear slightly forward of the other.

The strike came as a blur and the rabbit bounded straight up in the after-second of shock. The rattlesnake lay by, watching, waiting for her dinner to be ready.

Crow Mayor took to wing and turned toward home. The shadows of evening told him it was the hour to retire. He barely had time to reach the rookery before nightfall. The day had come and gone with no sign of the Coming. He reached his favorite roost and bumped a young upstart into space with his landing, removing the interloper.

Perhaps tomorrow. Definitely soon. This was the season, Mayor felt with growing conviction. Already the miracle had begun. He closed his eyes, calling on the lore of a thousand generations of prophets, tuning his mind to the universal wave from which all knowledge is derived. It was there somewhere, the isolated molecule that would deliver the Coming.

Crow Mayor stretched his wings and refolded them, fluffing the feathers to ward off mosquitoes. He took particular care to clamp his toes securely. He closed his eyes again. If he tried hard enough, surely he could find the one. Among millions, billions, trillions, one infinitesimal speck was the one he sought. At this moment it was like all the other molecules the world over. It was a time of propagation and regeneration.

It was the season of golden miracles.

II

"Is he dead?"

"I don't think so."

"Asleep, perhaps?"

"Nothing sleeps so soundly as that."

The flock gathered on every available inch of limb and twig, their voices hushed. Crow Mayor sat stone-still and stiff. His eyes were closed, his head pulled between his shoulders like a bird caught in a heavy rainfall. He had not awakened from the night's sleep.

"Could he be ill?"

"What illness makes one sleep like the deceased?"

A murmur of hoarse whispers swept the rookery.

"Well, come, come," an elder crow admonished, "we can't spend our day sitting here watching the old bird snooze. Pick two sentries to keep away predators and let the rest of us be about our business!"

So it was done. Two guards remained behind, one at the top

of the tree in which Crow Mayor slept, the other not much higher than Mayor himself. They fell silent and waited. Crow Mayor was not asleep. Not exactly. He had gone to sleep with his brain in neutral, tuned to the universal wave. He had been in search of that single molecule somewhere in the world that was to be the Coming of Crow Corvus. So intent was he on his quest that Crow Mayor quite forgot himself. He lost track of time and space.

It was a magnificent feeling! It was a sensation akin to meeting a sudden air pocket that thrusts you groundward, sending your heart into your craw. Or like flying along with your mind not on your pattern, and topping a rise to find yourself over a deep canyon a mile higher than you were a moment before.

Crow Mayor had entranced himself.

Many years ago, as a young bird, he had been captured by a Mexican family who took him into their home. It was his first experience with humans and he was deathly afraid. He would soon learn they meant him no harm, but in those first few days in the human house, surrounded by alien sounds and placed in a cage, Crow Mayor was sure he would die at their hands. The first time he entranced himself was almost an accident. He was perched in the human-made cage, human faces surrounding him as they gazed through the bars. He closed his eyes and willed himself elsewhere.

"Muerto, Papá?" the Mexican boy asked.

"Hasta la muerte todo es vida," the father replied. "Nobody is dying until he is dead."

The mother said, "The bird is in shock. He will soon be all right. For now, let us leave him alone."

Crow Mayor had heard their words and, surprisingly, entranced as he was, he could understand them! It was the first evidence he had of the universal wave.

13

Later, when the boy's father was killed in an accident, they sold Mayor to a pet shop in Mexico City, which in turn sold him to another pet shop in Tampico. Once again Mayor entranced himself, and soon found he could tap the minds of beasts, birds, and man; this plane of existence he called the universal wave. It was a means of acquiring information from any mind anywhere. He found that human language was useful. Human place names and even human terms for animal species were often more precise than the general descriptive phrases animals used.

Crow Mayor fled the Tampico pet shop at the first opportunity, in a raging storm that had knocked a tree through the skylight and broken his cage. The storm blew him for days, helter-skelter over the Gulf of Mexico with no land in sight. Ultimately, riding the tallest mast of an oil tanker, he had come to port in Mobile, Alabama—from whence he made his way to the rookery that had since been his home.

Last night, his mind seeking the atom of the Coming, he had drifted from his body and left the hull of himself perched on the roost. Little wonder the community thought him dead. His pulse, normally 140 to 150, had slowed to half that. His body temperature, which generally ranged between 103 and 112 degrees, had cooled to a chilly 64. He was as dead as a crow can be and still live. Nothing remained but the barely viable body. Crow Mayor himself, his mind and soul, had gone seeking the Coming.

When entranced, Crow Mayor could go anywhere. *Anywhere.* He could pierce the thickest nest of wasps, walk the beds of swirling rivers, penetrate the mound of an anthill, or actually enter the body of another animal and follow the flow of that creature's blood. He could be someplace, or anyplace, or everywhere at once.

The miracle was taking place everywhere. Four miles high

14

in a jet stream blowing bits of spiderweb—the miracle was there. Atop towering mountains, on the frozen plains of the arctic, deep in caves, everywhere Crow Mayor looked in the world, hundreds of billions of eggs were waiting to hatch. Birds, fish, amphibians, insects, and reptiles all had one thing in common—eggs.

Millions of fish, crabs, sea horses, clams, pond snails, frogs, and other amphibians had watery nests for countless billions of eggs. The chances for survival of a baby newly hatched underwater were slim. For that reason, aquatic creatures were the world's champion egg-layers. A codfish laid four to six million eggs at a single spawning as Mayor watched, invisible. A seventeen-pound turbot had nine million eggs, and a fifty-pound ling had more than twenty-eight millions eggs! The lowly oyster topped them all by laying sixty million eggs each year. If every egg hatched and survived for only one year, all the waters of the earth would be a writhing tangle of life. Actually, Mayor learned, less than one egg in a million needed to survive to keep such species plentiful.

Snakes, turtles, lizards, alligators, and crocodiles were laying eggs. Shells with leathery coverings, the reptile eggs were usually oblong and buried in moist, warm sand. Some reptile mothers such as the rattlesnake carried the eggs in their bodies until a few minutes before the eggs hatched, thereby giving more protection to the babies.

Crow Mayor discovered more than seven hundred thousand species of insects, almost all of which laid eggs. The insect mothers ranged in size from a fifteen-inch long "walking stick" insect of the tropics to insects so small they could not be seen except by humans with powerful microscopes.

There were only two mammals which laid eggs—the duckbill platypus and the echidna of Australia—although nearly all life began as an "egg" in some form.

One million two hundred thousand species of reptiles, mammals, birds, fish, insects, amphibians, worms, and snails laid eggs. The method of fertilization and incubation varied with each species. It would take a million days to tell each species' habit of nesting, breeding, and protection of their young.

It was then that Mayor discovered a cardinal rule: the egg—the egg itself and its development—was much the same with all forms of life. It was an exciting and awesome truth, and it so enthralled Crow Mayor that he completely forgot his body, which was still roosting on a limb back at the rookery.

When the community returned, the two sentries reported that Crow Mayor's body had not moved so much as a pinfeather as they guarded it.

"Then he is dead," someone stated.

"I don't think so," a sentry replied.

"If he does not move and he doesn't seem to be breathing," an elder crow said, "he must surely be dead!"

"I really don't think so," the sentry persisted.

"Impertinent upstart!" the elder snapped. "What evidence have you that the old bird isn't deceased?"

"Get very close to his body," the sentry said.

"Close to the body?"

"Yes, and everyone must be absolutely quiet."

The rookery hushed as the elder crow hesitantly inched sidewise along the limb to get next to Crow Mayor's stilled form.

"Well?" the elder demanded of the sentry.

"Don't you hear it?"

"Hear it?" the elder said. "Hear what?"

"Listen!"

They held their breath. Even at distances which would have prevented them hearing Mayor had he been speaking aloud, they held their breath, listening. Not a feather rustled. The elder leaned toward Mayor's motionless body, his head extending farther and farther out until the feathers on his neck were standing apart on taut flesh. He listened. And he heard it.

A hum.

That's what he heard. A hum. Like the hum of a bee in a lily as the insect attempts to back out with pollen-laden legs. Or like the hum in the copper wires on high-tension lines strung between cities.

"Yes," the elder said wisely, "I do hear it."

"What is it?" someone whispered.

"I don't hear anything," said another.

"Quiet!"

They hushed again, and again the elder listened. It was there, all right—a hum. Dead things generally don't sit perched on a limb. But dead things certainly never hum!

"We will post sentries for so long as is necessary for our esteemed Crow Mayor to awaken," the elder announced. "Or until he quits humming. Whichever comes first."

Crow Mayor was totally unaware of the hubbub taking place around his body back at the roost.

Deep in the body of a baby female chick lies a single egg cell. By the time the chick is barely three months old, this cell has been joined by thousands like it—many thousands more than the mature hen will ever use. Even before the chick is four months of age, the egg begins its journey. In all fowl of the world the journey is the same—the same process, the same timing. Crow Mayor began where the egg began, choosing one single egg cell. He determined not to lose sight of that one.

Mayor joined the cell. He examined his surroundings. It

was warm, moist, and secure around the area of the egg cell. Even though carried by a baby still in the nest, a first rich layer of yolk had already covered the cell before the female carrier was thirteen weeks old. The egg—the cell with its yolk—was at this point so small that only a microscope would show it to the human eye.

The egg's makeup became more complex as it increased in size. The single cell Mayor was following did not change; it had to be fertilized and heated to exactly the right temperature before it would become a growing thing.

The cell was getting daily applications of thick yolk. The yolk was not a "simple" yellow mass; it was made up of six layers, and each layer had a yellow and white portion carefully wrapped around the cell within. The coating of yolk was formed on a strict schedule guided by the position of the sun, which induced the female bird's body to produce the yolk. The yellow was produced during the daylight hours and stopped before midnight. The white layers of the yolk were produced between midnight and dawn.

A final layer of yolk engulfed the egg cell when the female bird realized that spring had arrived, and that it was time to build a nest. Mayor learned that mating was necessary for the crows and other wild birds to produce eggs, but that no male need be around the ducks, geese, turkeys, and chickens of the barnyard, which automatically begin laying at maturity.

As he continued his search, Mayor learned another cardinal rule: birds fall into two types. One type lays a specific number of eggs and stops, no matter what happens to them. The other type keeps laying eggs if some are stolen or broken, until there are the number of eggs in the nest which her species requires before starting to "brood"—to incubate the eggs.

When courting occurred, the egg cell, encased in six layers

18

of yolk, pulled away from its tie next to hundreds of other developing eggs. The egg traveled down a tube called the oviduct, where the egg was fertilized. Despite himself, Mayor was moved to cheer this event unseen by any eyes but his and God's. At that awesome moment, the egg became more than a single cell among many cells. Now it was potentially a new life.

The egg adhered to a precise schedule. It stopped in the oviduct for twenty minutes while it gathered albumen. Like the yolk, the white albumen was composed of layers. The first layer was thin. The second layer was stretchable, tough, and had the purpose of protecting the fragile cell in the yolk from changes in temperature and from being bounced around.

On down the oviduct went the egg, twisting as it moved. The motion served two purposes: to press a thin watery mass of albumen around the yolk, holding it more or less in the center. This "cord" would later break, and the mother bird would have to turn her eggs in the nest to keep the yolk from rising to one extreme edge of the shell. The cell would seek the highest point atop the yolk, floating in watery albumen and held within the tough outer layer of albumen applied earlier.

Two more elastic layers of albumen were now placed around the egg. It took more than two hours for the bird's body to produce and apply those last two layers. Even now the egg was still soft and easily bent. It was ready for the shell, which would go on in four porous layers of limy solutions. Outside, in the world, the time was late afternoon. Through the night the shell was applied, and with it the distinctive colors which mark most birds' eggs. In the case of the crow, the egg's color might be bluish green or olive buff, with irregular markings of brown and grey. Depending on the species, the eggs of other birds may be pure white, solid brown or black, deep blue, pastel colors, streaked, lined, mottled or, like the crow's, blotched.

Crow Mayor was startled. The egg had paused. Something momentous was about to occur and, for an instant, Mayor felt fear, something he had never experienced while entranced. What was there to fear while he was in this state? Nothing could touch him, nothing could harm him inside this young female crow's body. Still, he could not deny the quaking terror that threatened to overwhelm him at this moment.

He searched desperately for a haven, a cove to hide him from this nameless threat. The egg! Of course! He pulled himself within, drawing his being from all places, sucking in the tendrils of thought and covering himself inside the temporarily motionless egg. Behind the shell, inside the yolk, within the fertilized cell, what could reach him here? Nothing. He was safe. It was warm, dark, pleasant, secure, peaceful, and quiet.

"He's dead I tell you!"

"It's still humming, isn't it?"

"Nonetheless, no crow could go this long without food. He's dead!"

"I tell you he is not dead! So long as there is a humming, we will not dispose of the body."

The rookery was divided now. Rains had come and drenched the stock-still body of Crow Mayor. A few tail feathers had fallen and exposed a nub of pale white flesh. The eyes were sunken as though the orbs had vanished behind closed lids. Yet the body sat there, feet tightly clamped, the low hum still clearly heard by all who took the trouble to listen.

"He should be cast down!" someone declared. "This is upsetting the entire rookery. Anyone can see he's surely dead."

"Then," the defender challenged, "how do you account for the hum?"

Yes, the hum.

That couldn't be denied.

So they did nothing but fret and continue to guard the inert and disturbing thing they knew as "Crow Mayor."

III

The female crow stood. A moment later an egg lay glistening in her nest, the moisture quickly drying, leaving the shell a duller hue. Crow Mayor discerned light through the eggshell, the warm light of a spring morning, when the mother left the nest. It darkened again when she returned. Around the cell were the golden yolk and layers of albumen. Still the fertilized cell had not changed. It was awaiting the touch of the mother's warm body to heat this inner sanctum to 99.5 degrees.

At last the quota was reached: unseen beside this egg were other eggs also waiting.

The mother's body, rushing to prepare her for the nesting, had allowed bald "brood spots" to appear on her underside so that, when she settled on the nest, no feathers would keep her body heat from reaching the precious eggs.

Slowly the temperature rose, and Crow Mayor experienced a jumbling, turning sensation which was caused by the mother crow as she regularly turned the eggs. Then, miraculously,

22

the still, silent world of the egg began to change—and Mayor began to change with it.

The cell divided in half and each half divided again. Over and over this division took place, and long lines of deep red blood vessels sprouted out from the cell to all parts of the yolk—for indeed, this yellow mass was the sole source of food for Mayor.

Air entered through pores of the eggshell. The white body of watery albumen took all wastes from this growing baby and delivered them out the same pores as gases.

In a remarkably short period, the original speck had grown dramatically in size. Had the egg been broken—which fortunately it was not—the speck would have been visible. Crow Mayor was changing daily, growing, curving, turning as nature created in miniature a likeness of the parent. Crow Mayor knew that if the world outside got too cold or hot, too dry or wet, the process would come to a halt and never begin again. Or if the shell cracked for any reason, the miracle would vanish and this new life would perish.

The albumen gave way and diminished, and the yolk was drawn within as the miracle progressed. An air sac developed at the blunt end of the egg where the baby's head would rest, allowing it to breathe when its lungs were fully developed.

He had a long wait in close confinement. Crow Mayor passed this time of entrancement visiting other eggs of other creatures. The development was much the same, although the rate of growth was different. Within a mother rattlesnake he discovered twelve eggs of tissue-thin sacs, each holding a baby snake complete with venom and fangs. On one of the baby rattlers he saw a single scale atop the infant's head that was absolutely white. The baby was still not completely formed and the day of birth was some time in the future, but Mayor took the white scale as a sign.

Deep in the body of an armadillo he discovered that a single cell had split! Now four identical babies were developing from that one cell, each precisely the same as his brothers and, of course, all males. In yet another armadillo he found the same division, and these were all females. He added another cardinal rule: there is no statement that is always correct. All eggs and the development of all eggs was the same. Yet with the armadillo, each original cell became four and the babies were nourished from a common placenta. All eggs and the development of all eggs was the same—but no statement is always correct.

A mother raccoon prepared a home for the coming birth of two babies. In the hollow of a rotted tree she placed leaves and lined the nest with fur from her own body. Atop the head of one baby was a patch of white, and Mayor took this as a sign.

He had been so busy thinking about the four identical quadruplets within the armadillo that he had failed to see another sign: each had a white birthmark in the very center of his forehead.

Enough! Mayor knew he must return to his own body. He pulled himself into one being, withdrawing from the areas his entranced mind had visited. Into the single cell of the developing egg, he mustered his being into one unit, the essence of the creature the world knew as Crow Mayor. Now to return to his physical body perched on the limb.

The egg tumbled under the mother's turning. Inside, Mayor had to reassimilate his powers of concentration. Back to his own body . . . A shiver traced the egg in which he dwelled and Mayor exhorted himself. Try again! With rising alarm he forced himself to pull free.

Exhausted, he struggled again and again to extricate himself, to be free of the egg, to go back to his own shell of skin, meat, bone, and feathers.

In that final split second of awareness, he saw the prophecy unfolding. To give himself, his knowledge, his protection to the Coming of Crow Corvus—he must die. That is how he would transmit all that was himself into the new being. With a sigh unheard by any mind but his own, Mayor relaxed. He had done all he was destined to do.

"This is disgusting," a crow harped. "I have never seen such wanton disregard for the deceased as this rookery is displaying! Is anyone going to deny that he is dead now?"

They had gathered in the tree adjoining and the flock sat gazing at the upside-down body of Crow Mayor, hanging by a single leg.

"Now, now," an elder cautioned, "we've all seen Crow Mayor do that from time to time. There isn't a bird present who can deny that Mayor has some—ah—unusual affectations."

"What about our babies?" a mother crow wailed. "What kind of community are we bringing them into? I don't want my nestlings to see that decaying creature hanging there!"

"How about the hum?" a crow asked.

"Yes, the hum. How about the hum?"

There was a breeze stirring the trees, so they had to wait for that to die down. Then an elder crow hop-stepped along Crow Mayor's limb to the place where the body hung. The elder had to flutter his wings to position himself so he could lean near and listen.

They all listened. The elder's tail flicked up, down, up, down, as he tried to balance himself with his posterior elevated at an angle which induced titters in the less tactful members of the rookery.

"Quiet, crabdabble it! I can't hear with all that snickering and whispering!"

25

Mothers shushed fledglings and silence reigned once more.

"Well?" somebody demanded.

"Hold your beaks, will you?" the listening elder commanded.

Silence.

The elder crow was nearly hung upside-down himself in his effort to hear. Then, with an awkward flapping, he remounted the limb and stepped away from Crow Mayor. He faced the flock and his gaze covered the expanse of the community. They waited, hushed.

"Crow Mayor," the elder pronounced, "is dead."

Indeed, he was. As the first full breath entered the body of the naked crow within the egg, Mayor's memory had vanished. Gone was his past, his years of accumulated experience. His final thought had been a question: Must it all be learned anew?

Perhaps it was the shaking of the limb on which Crow Mayor had always roosted; many crows later said that was what did it. Or perhaps it was merely coincidence. But at the exact moment when the elder crow announced Mayor's death as final, the body dropped like a feathered stone to the sod below, where it landed with an uncommonly light thud.

"Dead?"

It was as though, despite the obvious, they could not believe it.

"Crow Mayor dead?"

"He was a fine bird," another elder stated.

"Indeed."

The flock began to break away, each going on his morning rounds in search of sustenance. By the silence of their departing, they made evident the respect Crow Mayor had earned over the many years of his life. The strange crow with a foreign accent had left his mark on the rookery.

* * *

On a morning eleven to eighty days after the egg is laid, depending on the species of bird, a faint cheep of a new voice comes from within the shell, and the feeble efforts of the young make the eggs rock slightly in the nest. At this point the mother seems to realize that this is *her* baby! The shell cracks and from one hour to one day later, after much strenuous work, the baby peeps out into the blinding light, rests, waits, gathers strength, and pushes itself free of the confinement of the shell.

The baby may be of a species that can leap up at once and dash away to water, such as ducks and geese do. Or the baby may be naked and helpless, with a terrific appetite that will keep its parents running for weeks as it develops strength and feathers and size. Whatever the next step, whatever infancy may bring, this baby—like all the hundreds of millions of babies in nests around the world—has begun its existence as a God-touched golden speck in the season of miracles.

In the burrow of a gopher turtle, several feet below ground, the mother armadillo brought forth her four identical sons. Beneath a log on a sandy patch of soil hidden by a palmetto frond, the mother rattlesnake delivered her dozen infants in the thin-shelled eggs which hatched a few moments later. Ten of these died on the spot as an alert hawk swooped down to devour them. Of the two which escaped, neither saw the mother. In the way of reptiles, she had abandoned her babies to fend for themselves or die. One of the survivors had a single white scale in the center of his triangular forehead. He slid beneath a cover of fallen leaves and thereby eluded the hawk. His brother, caring nothing for parent or sibling, was gone in a different direction.

As for the raccoon, the most maternal of them all, she licked clean her two babies, taking no particular notice of any

27

unusual markings on the furry tads. The blemish on the forehead of one was correctly assumed to be a birthmark. To her it meant nothing.

Of the four eggs in the crow's nest, three hatched. The other was eventually pushed out by the mother as a miscarried effort. Between the mother and father, scrambling to secure food for three gaping mouths was a full-time occupation for the next several weeks. Each baby would require ten ounces of food daily, consuming a staggering 13½ pounds each in three weeks of nest life—at which time each baby would weigh about a pound. With over forty pounds of food to acquire and transport, the harried parents were kept hunting constantly. They returned to find those insistent mouths wide, heads waggling, each baby elbowing the others aside as he struggled to dominate the food train.

Upon alighting, the parent responds to the widest mouth. It is this and no other stimulus which makes the parent select a given chasm to fill. If the infant is less hungry, he is less insistent and his mouth less wide. The hungriest is thereby assured of food with a system of rotation superb in its simplicity and accuracy.

In this particular nest a tragic but not uncommon occurrence took place. On the third day after hatching, the first baby nudged one of his nestmates over the side to death below. A few days later, the second baby was dislodged, leaving but one of the original three. Mercifully, parents in the wild are blessed with short memories of their young. A certain number die; it's a cardinal rule. There's no point in grieving—it's bound to happen. As for the remaining bird, he was well fed and more closely cared for.

A mother bird is driven by instinct, but crows are not slaves to instinct alone. Among the most intelligent of all birds, they adapt quickly to new situations. Therefore, when the mother paused to scrutinize her last remaining baby and noticed a single white feather in its crown, she immediately plucked it out. Being different invited trial. She was not about to surrender her final fledgling because of a single inappropriate feather!

The infant crow learned rapidly. More silent than most nestlings, he gave voice infrequently and his tone carried an authority rarely heard in fledglings. Or was this merely a mother's pride that made her think so? Of the seven seasons and twenty babies she had seen take wing, this baby was unique. He did not have to be enticed from the nest. Nor did she have to shove him squawking from the limb to test his wings. He took off naturally, quickly, with no protest. True, he floundered and landed badly, but learning takes time. He stood on the ground and flexed his wings, as though testing the muscles.

"Fly! Fly!" mothers around the rookery were screaming at their charges.

"Get your lazy tail off that limb, boy! Fly! Let go of that twig. Here, boy! Get off!"

The mother crow settled on the ground beside her baby and cocked her head quizzically, questioning.

"I'm all right," he said softly.

"You did very well for the first time."

"The muscles must learn," her baby said.

"The muscles must—what grown-up talk for a fledgling!"

He looked at her steadily for a long moment, then ran along the ground, gaining speed, holding out his wings, rising a few feet, coasting, and alighting again. She flew to a low limb to observe and guard the infant, as did all the members of the community, ever alert for predators.

Ow! He smacked into a stump. She saw him shake his head and gamely undertake the effort anew. Running, flapping his wings, rising to glide, he made a far better landing this time.

"Good!" she crowed. "Very good. Keep at it."

Babies all over the rookery were bawling to their mothers, "Get me, get me, get me!"

"Fly! Fly! Would you look at that? Get your wings up, stupid. Look at that! Right into the bushes. Don't just hang there—get out and fly!"

"Mother?"

She dropped down beside him.

"I've forgotten," he said. "Do you fan the wings to break a downdraft, or close them?"

"Close the feathers to stay up, open to go down," she responded automatically. She cocked her head at him. "What do you mean, you forgot?"

He was not sure what he had meant, so he did not reply, but rose with labored beatings of the wings to a low limb where he sat for a few moments resting his strained muscles. He gave a quick hop and beat his wings more surely and rose a little higher. The mother followed at a discreet distance, watching, her breast filled with immense pride. Her fledgling was large. His feathers had a magnificent sheen, his eyes were alert and steady, and his bill was strong. He moved with a sureness that would ultimately make him a leader. It might be pride, but this baby—her baby—was different!

She watched him, after a single day of practice, reach the very pinnacle of a pine. His voice rang sharp and true: "Cawt! Cawt! Cawt!"

The rookery fell silent as the sound of his voice caromed across the woodland. All eyes turned to him and the young

30

crow flapped his wings, holding tight to his perch to keep anchored as he asserted himself. "Cawt! Cawt! Cawt!" he challenged again.

No fledgling had ever done this before. No young crow would dare assert himself in such a manner. The other crows did not know why it disturbed them, but it did. It was a sign. That they knew.

IV

It was a time of learning, and Crow took his lessons well. Overcoming a natural curiosity, he soon learned the value of patience, careful study of an area before alighting, and a sharp eye on the horizon.

The crows had more than good sense. They were wily, adaptable birds. From infancy they practiced matching wits through thievery. It was expected of them. If a neighbor was building a nest, it was permissible to steal her sticks. If a fellow crow found a particularly interesting trinket and brought it home to store with other accumulated gems, the cache was fair game to the crow that could lift it and get away.

There were penalties, of course. If caught in the act of pilfering, one could anticipate a hard rap on the skull by a chisel-sharp beak. He could also expect to be hooted out of the rookery by his peers, the subject of snide caws and open chuckles until he redeemed himself and regained his honor in some way. Stealing was a way of life, quite socially acceptable, but one must do it well.

For a few glorious weeks the number of birds in the world doubled or tripled. During the time of hatching, fields were being plowed by man, and unearthed grubs and worms were plentiful. Swarms of insects were everywhere. There was food aplenty. Then came the inevitable scythe of equalization, eliminating the sick, injured, old, and unwary.

Death came in many guises: disease, parasites, hunger, and plain bad luck. The first year of life was the most hazardous. The fledglings were armed only with an intuitive caution, lacking the wisdom of experience. Millions would die before the surviving witnesses gained the keen edge of alertness necessary to live.

They ate almost anything: carrion, fruits, berries, nuts, the eggs of other birds, rodents, small reptiles, seeds, and insects. But as summer came on, things began to change. Insects came into check; the farmer's crops were up but not yet yielding fruit. When a scout found a field abounding in grasshoppers, the flock would rise at dawn and travel as far as forty miles to feast, returning that night to the rookery.

Crow, too, was caught in the ceaseless search for food. Burning tremendous quantities of fuel was essential for the herculean task of flying. Twenty-five percent of his total weight was found in the powerful breast muscles needed for flight. Lacking sweat glands to cool this flying machine, air sacs were spread throughout every important part of his body. Therefore, he used the air he breathed more efficiently than any mammal. The sacs also dissipated the enormous volume of heat generated by the energy expended in air travel.

Food for the crow was required in huge quantities, needed daily, even hourly. A fast of a few days might render him so weak he could not forage. The odds for survival of a lone bird, the flock, or an entire species could alter in a single season. By the spring of the next year, the global population of birds would be almost exactly the same as the year before— one hundred billion.

Despite the relentless need for food, Crow was obsessed with a desire to explore. Often sacrificing the immediate necessity of body fuel, he took time to wander for the pleasure of wandering. From hardwoodlands to coniferous forests to seashore he traveled. Upon discovering a strange creature, he ventured as near as prudence would allow, often suffering its abuse and disdain. He quickly learned the value of a low silhouette and silence when in strange surroundings. The thrill of garnering new knowledge often had to be sacrificed to the work of getting food, time for which he resented. He soon deduced that the more time a creature had free from the pressures of feeding, the more highly developed the animal was likely to be. A ravenous hunger left little room for other considerations.

He thought these thoughts sitting at the edge of a bayou, watching the sun sink beyond the laced fingers of cypress trees shrouded with moss. His reason for being here, when he should be going home, was a sight he had never observed before. A mother raccoon had ambled out of a dead tree, followed by two kittens. The young raccoons waddled about on the moist sand and mud bank of the bayou creek as the mother waded belly deep in water, fishing for crawdads. She held her chin up, hands pumping as she used her sense of touch to locate anything edible. Upon finding it, she would lift it, bite it to render the crustacean helpless and immediately stick the creature back in the water to wash it!

Bemused by the washing of that which lives in water, Crow, like the mother raccoon, failed to see tragedy in the making.

So silently came the bobcat, they neither heard nor saw it. Placing his padded feet carefully, head down, the short-tailed feline moved with claws retracted. Every hair of the cat's body gave her a message, and she automatically sidestepped where necessary to avoid rustling a single leaf. Each rear foot assumed the tested print of the forepaw before it. No twig snapped. Like a tawny shadow, the cat was drawn to the chirring of the kittens as they played, and to the splashing sounds of the mother raccoon going about her business of foraging.

Hiding behind the last shred of vegetation, the cat paused, every muscle tensed, crouching for the final dash. Unseen by all, she judged distance, timing, and the probability of success. She selected her prey, one of the babies, and bounded.

Crow involuntarily flapped his wings as though to fly, but did not leave the limb. The cat's fangs struck home and with a single cry the infant was finished. Instantly the other baby streaked for cover and the mother raccoon raced at the cat.

By far the superior of the two, the bobcat could have defeated the raccoon mother, but it would have taken a fight. One fights only when one must, however; no matter how trivial the injury, it is a step toward disease, deprivation, and death. The bobcat elected to retreat, prey in mouth, leaving the horrified parent circling in shock, seeking her young.

Mother and survivor met, touching noses, and she caressed the baby's face as though to be sure it was truly there. The two of them chirped vocal assurances in the way raccoons do when they fondle one another. A dead limb nearby chose this instant to fall and the mother wheeled, hair on end, teeth bared, placing her last baby behind her to ward off an attacker. There was no attacker.

Obviously shaken, mother and baby moved downstream, the mother looking back, circling as though to return now and then, as if she might have made a mistake and her other baby would still be there somewhere, waiting to be found.

Crow took wing, turning toward the rookery. Only a few minutes of light remained and he was not a night bird. He propelled himself with urgency. He had to settle for a strange roost on a far side of the rookery which he had never frequented. There, among very casual acquaintances, he spent the night dozing, awakening fitfully, thinking of life and its brevity.

"If you've going to continue these foolhardy expeditions, the least you might do is get home before nightfall!" His mother was angry, but it was an emotion born of fear.

"I'm sorry."

"I don't want to command you," she said sharply. "I would prefer to appeal to your reason. But you are giving me no choice. If you persist in endangering yourself, I will take it up with the elders. Do you understand?"

"I understand."

Less tartly she asked, "What do you do all day?"

"I look around."

"Look at what?"

"Everything."

"What do you see?"

"The world, mother."

"What do you eat?"

"Whatever I can find."

"You're missing the melon season. Cantaloupes are ripening and yesterday we had a feast. I'm sorry you weren't there."

"It's all right."

"No, son, it isn't. You need to remain with the flock. If a sin found you alone, you wouldn't stand a chance. There is security in having sentries and fellow crows to help if you run into trouble."

"There are no sins out in daylight, mother."

36

"Very well," she snapped, "then fear the hawks!"

"Mother," he said softly, "must I fear anything?"

"Perhaps fear is a poor choice of words. Be wary of hawks, I should say."

"I would think the sins would be more dangerous than hawks, since they attack at night when we can't see."

She combed her feathers nervously, in the manner of any parent under scrutiny by her progeny. "I keep telling you, there's safety in numbers. No sin attacks a compact rookery. They wouldn't dare! It's the strays, sick, and negligent which get caught by sins."

"I'll be more careful about returning nights," he conceded.

It was a compromise and she accepted. He had no intention of halting his lone excursions. To appease her, he went with the flock the following morning to a field speckled with golden cantaloupes.

He met the quadruplets quite by accident. Walking the furrows of a harvested cornfield, Crow was attracted to a burrow by the sounds of digging. He stood atop a mound of fresh dirt, his feet cooling in the moist loam, looking into a black hole from which the scratching sounds were coming.

What came out of there was startling and strange. First a long shielded tail emerged, followed by a rounded and practically hairless shell-like covering of armor, and finally a head with a pointed snout and two small beady eyes.

"What are you?" Crow asked.

"A f-fourth."

"Aforth?"

"*One* f-fourth," the armadillo corrected. "I'm a f-fourth of the f-family."

Thereupon, out of the same burrow backed an exact duplicate of the first animal. Shortly thereafter, two more were beside these two, and all four stood staring at Crow with the pinched expression common among myopic beasts.

"By what name do I call you?" Crow asked.

"Name?" they asked in unison.

"Do you know yourselves by name?"

"We are an armadillo."

"Each of you is an armadillo," Crow said. "It doesn't take all of you to make a whole."

Crow deliberated, then announced, "I'll call you Dill. Each of you as individuals and all of you as a group, since I can't tell you apart anyway. Is that all right?"

"Perfectly!" the four of them chorused. In fact, the idea seemed to have great appeal.

"Say," they said, "do you mind if we have a closer look at you? We don't see too well at a distance, particularly in bright light."

Crow debated the advisability of close inspection and decided to chance it. The quadruplets waddled forward on short legs, and Crow saw at once that their undersides were soft and fleshy.

"Ouch!" Crow said, as one of them pulled at a tail feather. In return for this he pecked the offender on the back and all four of them yelled, "Ouch!"

"All of you felt that peck?" Crow asked.

"Quadruplets are sensitive to the feels of their brothers," he was informed haughtily. Crow was amazed to see that his attack had brought forth blood.

"I'm sorry," he apologized. "I pecked so hard because I thought your shell was hard."

"It is hard," they said, "but it's still skin. We scratch like everything else."

"I assumed it was like a turtle shell," Crow said.

"No," they chorused.

"Why do all of you speak at the same time?" Crow demanded. "Can't you think for yourselves?"

They squinted at one another for a second and then with great effort, one alone spoke, his voice hesitant. "It-it mu-mu-makes it easier to spu-sp-speak together, for some reason."

This was unusual for armadillos, Crow soon learned. Although armadillos are born as quadruplets and any litter is always either all females or all males, they don't normally stay together. After weaning they go their separate ways. But these four were different. Alone, each of them stuttered and stammered and seemed unsure of himself. Together, as a unit, they thought much better and communicated far more easily. In time, Crow came to think of them as one and when he said "Dill" he spoke to them as a group, not as individuals.

He also found that armadillos are really not very smart. Evidently it took four together to pool enough intelligence to converse clearly.

Dill proved to be a pleasant and comfortable companion. Crow tried to get by their burrow at least once or twice a week just to be cordial. As in all satisfying relationships, they did not find it necessary to chatter constantly to enjoy one another. Crow would perch overhead and preen his feathers, weaving the filaments back together after a rough flight, as Dill busily extended his burrow, or whatever.

Dill was also Crow's first relationship with a creature that was not of his own kind. That pleased him, too. He had been friends with Dill for some weeks when it finally occurred to the armadillos to ask, "What name have you, now that we are called 'Dill'?"

"Name? I am a crow," he said.

"That's what you *are,*" they said in unison. "But that isn't your name!"

"It is customary for a crow to name himself only if he

survives to his first hatchday," Crow advised them. "Having decided on a name, he proclaims it to the rookery."

"Have you decided on a name for yourself?"

It came as a mild surprise to Crow that, indeed, he had not given it so much as a passing thought. To his mother he was "son" and to the rookery he was "fledgling" or, because of his immense size, strange crows sometimes called him "yearling." There had been no particular name required, since this satisfied the needs of his existence within the community.

"I don't know what I will call myself," Crow confessed.

Dill mused over this, proffering various suggestions, none of which gave Crow any ideas.

"How about Streaker?" they suggested.

"Uh—no," Crow said.

"Or Blacky?"

"I'll have to think about it a while," Crow said tactfully.

"Say, what do you think about Swifty?" they chorused.

"Or Speedy?"

"It's going to require some thought, I think," Crow suggested.

"Don't suppose you'd like Beaker?"

"It doesn't strike me right, no."

The armadillos were quite involved in their game, exercising their collective imagination, and Crow finally took his leave with them still sending up suggestions.

That evening, as he settled on the roost, Crow turned to his mother.

"By what name shall I call myself?"

"That's a decision you must make, son."

"I want it to be appropriate, with dignity."

"There's plenty of time left for that decision," she said sleepily. She was looking at him through half-closed nictitating membranes, her head pulled deep between her shoulders.

"I want a good name," he said.

"It'll come to you. Don't worry about it."

He went to sleep pondering names, weighing them, testing them mentally.

V

Crow spent several pleasant hours each week conversing with Dill. It surprised him to learn that no other crow had ever talked with armadillos. In fact, his fellow crows could not even comprehend the language of other species of birds! Of course, all crows knew certain communications. The distinctive screech of a distressed bluejay was a cry that all birds understood. The sound of some species calling their flocks to a food supply would often be answered by the crows themselves. But there was no flow of ideas and thoughts between crows and other creatures.

Crow found that each race of beings transmitted messages in distinctive ways. Dill told him that odors were used by some animals as a means of letting others of their own kind know of their presence. This was a mystery to Crow, whose sense of smell was very weak. Dill said the use of scents either attracted or repelled as the perfumer desired. The use of odors ranged from "stink" bugs and skunks using their acrid fumes to drive away enemies, to animals that used a musky essence to attract a companion. However, Crow did not really consider the use of odor as "communicating."

"And if it is," Crow explained to Dill, "it would be more of an announcement than a conversation. Like a scream of danger which we all recognize no matter what the source."

"But, Crow," Dill chorused, "we don't talk to anything but armadillos—and you!"

Thereupon Crow began to study communications. He now paid close attention to other creatures in the act of speaking to one another. Surprisingly, the most vocal orators seemed to transfer thoughts the least efficiently. As an example, he told Dill about the monotonous repetitions of the red-eyed vireo, a bird known to humans as the "preacher bird." That drab sparrow-sized relative of the wood warbler repeated the same tiresome phrases thousands of times a day. What did he say? Nothing! At least nothing worth hearing.

It was the same with other birds. Robins, mockingbirds, and hundreds of other so-called songbirds made a great variety of sounds. But all they were doing was staking out a territory and calling a mate. Talking with such birds was a crashing bore. There wasn't a creative thought in their heads. Crow had listened for hours as a tedious songbird told him the relative merits of blackberry brambles as opposed to other thickets for nesting. An inane kingfisher mother kept him fidgeting for an entire afternoon as she discussed the distance a parent should carry the shells of newly hatched eggs before dropping them.

Crow found that vocal sounds of birds revolved around several set subjects: food, predators and other foes, sexual behavior and aggressions stemming from it, or parent-infant relationships. It was true that some migrating birds made a

43

distinct sound heard only at night. But these migrant cries were for the purpose of keeping such transients in touch when they could not see one another.

None of this was "communicating" on the level that Crow enjoyed. Among members of his own rookery he recognized the fact that certain community members were more intelligent than others. All of the elders were smart—hence their survival, perhaps. Intelligence didn't seem to make communicating with other animals more likely. Nor did it necessarily increase a given crow's ability to communicate with another crow.

"Then how do we manage to talk to you?" Dill questioned, in consonance. "How do you speak to us?"

It was a good question, and Crow was not at all sure why or how it happened. His chats with Dill did not make use of physical signals. Nor did they use vocal sounds.

"I don't know how we do it," Dill offered soberly. They sat squinting at one another, pondering. Watching this, Crow suddenly cawed.

"I've got it! We communicate by thinking. When you started thinking, I could hear every word. That's why the four of you speak at precisely the same time. We're thinkers!"

"Thinkers?" Dill queried. "We're probably the first thinkers known to armadillodom. That's great! Thinkers."

And that was it. So simple. Yet impossible to teach any creatures who could not do it. Try as he might in years to come, Crow would never succeed in bridging the gap between crows and other birds unless he acted as interpreter. How he did it he could not know. All living things could do it—think, that is—but the level on which they thought varied. Like with a possum. There was the dumbest one animal that ever existed! Grinning and simpering, a possum was nature's prime example of stupidity.

Even with the possum, Crow communicated. Not often, but on occasion, Crow had bade "good morning" to a random possum on its way to bed with the coming of day.

Thereafter, Crow went out of his way to test his ability to communicate with various creatures. With hundreds of species of birds, he attempted conversations. Except with sparrows and their like, of course—those little flitters had no civility! They wore their animosity on their wings like the red badge of some blackbirds.

"What are you doing when you spend so much time staring at strange animals?" an elder once questioned Crow.

"Just looking."

"Looking for what?"

"Looking to see what they do and how they do it," Crow said. "Don't you ever watch things besides other crows and enemies?"

"Not for hours on end," the elder scoffed. "It's a waste of time. What good is to come of it?"

"Well, you never know," Crow replied, taking wing. "I might pick up something that would be useful sometime."

"Irresponsible fledgling," the elder grumbled, watching Crow depart with deliberate strokes of the wing.

Crow acquired knowledge beyond conversations. Around Dill, Crow "sensed" what a burrow was like. Although Dill had never discussed it, Crow knew the comfort musky damp soil gave Dill. He even knew the smell of it! A rich, moist, rooty odor, quite alien to him, but so pleasant to Dill that Crow drew pleasure from it, too.

From a seagull with whom Crow spent a day, he learned the feel of diving, a performance which gave the gull much enjoyment. If Crow had attempted such a show, he would have put a crack in his pectoral girdle. Or more likely he would have drowned.

It was one thing to wade in shallow creeks in search of crawdads. It was quite another to dive at the surface of the gulf for a fish. Yet Crow could understand how the gull did it and could fully appreciate why the gull enjoyed it. This he learned in a series of flickering images and emotions transmitted unknowingly by the gulls as they chatted about entirely different subjects.

These exchanges made Crow more tolerant of opposing viewpoints.

"You really shouldn't hate sparrows so much," Crow counseled a fledgling who was describing an attack he had suffered.

"Hate them?" the other crow shrilled. "I loathe them! Look at my tail. See those bare spots? I look like a molting oldest elder because those dirty little birds assaulted me. There must've been a hundred of them. Zoom! Zoom!" The offended crow crouched on a limb, demonstrating how the divers had soared in to snatch at his tendermost points.

"They do that," Crow explained softly, "because for centuries we crows have been robbing their nests and breaking their eggs."

"You mighty-be-crabdabbled-right!" the sore crow seethed. "And I'm going to crack as many eggs and tear up as many nests as I can, too! What are you, a sparrow-lover?"

An unpleasant current swept the listeners, and Crow saw the wisdom of backing down.

"Sparrow-lover?" Crow cackled. "Me? I'm the one they pinioned to an oak tree, remember? They nearly ruined my rudder! I'm just now growing back some of those tail feathers."

"Yeah, well," the injured crow said ominously, "I'd watch what I said about those little beggars, if I were you."

Crow agreed, adding an anecdote or two about his own

encounter with sparrows, exaggerating the battle and his wounds therefrom. At a propitious moment later, he took wing on the pretext of inspecting a late planting of tomatoes some distance away.

He would hereafter remember: prejudice seeks no relief.

That was the day he learned that no one, not even other crows, could detect his innermost thoughts. There he had been telling the suspicious crows about his imaginary attack by sparrows and they heard only those thoughts which Crow wished them to hear. Instantly he realized the power of this. Knowing or sensing what another creature felt and thought without having his own emotions betrayed was like stealing trinkets from a dying bird.

For lack of anything better to do, and with his craw already filled from a robust lunch of figs and seed grasses, Crow went looking for Dill. He found one of the quadruplets sleeping near the mouth of their burrow and woke him.

"Where're the others?" Crow inquired.

"D-d-down below. Asleep. I th-th-think."

"Would you like some carrion?" Crow asked. "I saw some at the far end of the field."

"S-s-sure!"

Crow walked beside the armadillo, chatting amiably and guiding his nearsighted friend to the food he had mentioned. It was just as well there was only one armadillo to be awakened, since the carrion wasn't very large.

Crow related the events of the hour before, as Dill dined. "I can't understand why there have to be fights that cause more fights," he said. "Crows and sparrows have been battling for generations. If we got together and agreed to leave one another alone, life would be far more pleasant for all."

"Mu-mu-maybe," the armadillo stammered, his mouth full, "but I d-d-doubt it. There'd always be that one c-c-crook who'd mess it up. He'd steal something. Or b-b-break a sparrow's eggs and it would j-j-just start all over again."

"Great grubs!" Crow exulted. "That's a pretty good thought. And you did it by yourself, Dill!"

The armadillo squinted his eyes and wiggled cup-shaped ears. "Yeah! I d-d-did, didn't I?"

That evening at the rookery, Crow arrived to assume his favorite roost and found an older yearling in his place. Rather than create a disturbance, Crow swerved away and circled, coming back to light on a nearby limb.

The older crow was surrounded by waves of belligerence. Such militant birds were usually trying to establish their place in the pecking order of the rookery. Crow had no desire to challenge this unknown just to verify his position. It was too late and he'd had enough nonsense about fighting for one day.

"You're that sparrow-lover, aren't you?"

Trouble can be confronted one of two ways. Run from it or face it. Run and the trouble's still there. A lesson Crow had already learned well was: deal with it and be done with it.

Without warning he swooped at the intruder and knocked the surprised bird for a loop, backward off the roost. Crow did not wait for a return attack. He was on the older bird all the way. They tumbled through the limbs of the tree with Crow delivering sharp, well-aimed rivets to the head of his adversary.

The whipped opponent was soon sent fleeing, the rookery hooting derisively at the shamed figure as he escaped in silence. Crow returned to his roost, acutely aware of the respect he had just acquired. He ruffled his feathers and took plenty of time to stretch his wings casually before settling down to clamp the limb and close his eyes.

The flock fell quiet, except for an occasional protest by a

bird being crowded on a communal roost here or there. The laughter ebbed away in diminishing waves and the light of day flowed away over the horizon, following the sun.

"I'm proud of you," his mother said softly.

"Thank you."

"You handled the matter very well," she added. "All afternoon they've been talking about you, calling you a sparrow-lover and other bad names. I was worried. Then when they sent that young tough over here, I became frightened."

"You don't need to worry about me, Mother."

"Perhaps not," she sighed. "But I do."

He heard her nestling down for the night, her thoughts becoming dreamy and peaceful. Crow breathed deeply and hunched his shoulders, pulling his head down. Despite his appearance of assurance and calm, his heart was racing. The bottoms of his feet were cold. He had faced and defeated the largest and meanest yearling in the rookery. Now with his mind closed to others, he recounted the event to himself in the most minute detail, remembering the flap of every wing and the crack of his beak on that crabdabbler's skull! He swelled with pride and chuckled to himself. He didn't want to boast to anyone else, but a little bragging to himself couldn't hurt. He thought about it, enjoying his victory over and over for as long as it took to go to sleep.

"It's fall," an elder observed grumpily. "I hate it."

"Why?" Crow asked.

"Before long the leaves will fall off the oak trees and we'll stand out like feathered knots on a log," the elder complained. "Pines are all right, but I'm an oak bird, myself."

"There are other hardwood trees," Crow noted.

"Not like an oak," the elder croaked. "Oaks have strength, majesty, security. In the summer, they do. In the winter, with all the leaves gone, they look disgustingly naked. Oaks shouldn't have to molt. It's a mistake for nature to make an oak take off its leaves every winter. They have such knobby joints."

"Most of us do, in a molt," Crow said.

The elder glared at Crow with stark black eyes. "You're a rare bird, fledgling. You show more sense than most of them. Reminds me of a friend I once had."

"Thank you," Crow said, genuinely pleased. Words of praise were rare from a crotchety elder.

The old bird shifted on arthritic legs, muttering, then settled again. The elder blinked slowly, the nictitating membrane of his inner eyelid not quite returning completely to the corners of his eyes. It was this clear film of flesh that cleansed and lubricated a bird's eye while still allowing him to see through it. To a bird, a blink that would shut off his vision could well invite disaster. With age, the muscles had weakened and the elder's inner eyelid did not recoil entirely, giving him a sleepy expression even when he was wide awake.

"I saw your fight last night," the elder said, his voice deep and crackling. "He called you a sparrow-lover."

Crow said nothing, fixing his gaze on a distant point to establish his humility.

The elder chuckled. "They once called my friend a 'sparrow-lover,' and he whipped five of the largest yearlings in the rookery. They never called him that again. But he *was* a—sparrow-lover. He said he didn't like them, but if he'd had his way, crows and sparrows would have made peace."

Keenly interested, Crow asked, "Who was this?"

The elder yawned, his pointed tongue protruding as he did so. "His name was Mayor," he said. "Crow Mayor."

VI

With the life-flow of sap slowed by winter, the curling leaves of the oaks were sucked dry, becoming crisp. Gone was the pliant greenery; in the throes of death, blanched and browned, the leaves lost their hold and wafted groundward. True to the elder's word, the oaks were gnarled and starkly grotesque in their nudity. The crows shifted their roosting patterns to avoid exposure, choosing instead the evergreens.

Eating patterns altered also. In search of insects, they walked the earth poking beneath twigs, small stones, and leafy blankets. For long hours the crows would sit in utter dejection, their plumage ruffled to trap body heat. This was a time of resourcefulness, a time to keep one's wits and be diligent in the quest for body fuel. Crow spent the better part of each day seeking sustenance. He counted the different things he and the other crows had taken for food, and it totaled a staggering 656 items! Of this, one-fourth was animal matter, the balance vegetable.

Hunger was a relentless master, making even the laziest of crows work for a living. The scarcity of food drove them apart, each bird seeking edibles as an individual rather than in a flock. Again, and more fervently than before, Crow cursed the need to seek food.

It had been weeks since he last saw Dill. When finally Crow did detour by the burrow of the armadillos, he half expected them to be gone. But there they were.

"We have company," Dill said collectively.

"Really?" Crow remarked. "What?"

"One surly turtle of the gopher variety," Dill snorted. "And one sleepy rattlesnake who has a short temper. We've been forced to extend our burrow to bypass them. They simply took over an entire chamber without so much as a how-do-you-do."

"Rattlesnake?" Crow questioned. "Aren't you afraid of him?"

"Oh, no," Dill said in unison. "Except for his grouchy nature, he's quite a decent serpent. Oh! And we talk to him!"

Crow did not seem impressed, so Dill repeated, with emphasis: "We *talk* to him, Crow! He can talk without words, because snakes make no sounds, so it has to be he's a thinker!"

"He makes no sounds?" Crow asked, his interest mounting.

"No sound except a hiss," Dill corrected. "And a rattle. He gets rattled easily."

"What does he talk about?" Crow persisted.

"Snake things mostly," Dill said. "He said he had to get in the burrow or he would die. He said his blood goes slower when he gets colder."

Thinking of the life-blood of trees, and the leaves falling off for lack of sap, Crow asked, "Do his scales fall off when his blood slows down?"

Dill giggled, a quartet of titters. "No!" Dill said. "He merely stops moving. The turtle has the same problem, evidently. Sits there icy-eyed like he's dead."

"Maybe he is dead," Crow speculated.

"No," Dill countered. "We nipped his tail and he moved. Not fast, but he moved. He's alive. But it's downright morbid. We've got lizards down there, too. The rattlesnake says it's because they're all cold-blooded."

"Cold-blooded?" Crow shuddered.

"That means their bodies don't make their own warmth. They're the same temperature inside as it happens to be outside. It's called 'cold-blooded,' though he says that isn't very accurate when it's very hot out."

"Cold-blooded," Crow mused. "Doesn't sound very inviting. Why don't you fellows move to a new burrow?"

Dill considered this novel approach to their problem, then negated it. "It's home," they decided, "so we'll stay."

"Have these tenants given any indication as to when they'll vacate the premises?" Crow inquired.

"Not a sign," Dill grumped. "The rattlesnake says he's not old enough to know what happens next. The turtle is either dulled by slow blood or dull by nature, but we can't get a thing out of him. He just sits there like a lump."

"How do you know you can trust the snake?" Crow asked.

"He's very reassuring, actually," Dill noted. "He seemed as pleased to talk to us as we were to discover he could communicate! He says being a snake is a very lonely business, especially a rattlesnake. It appears that he doesn't have too many friends. I think he likes us."

"While he's feeling lonely," Crow suggested. "I'd find out what he eats when he's not so lonely."

"Not us," Dill said with finality. "He's like you, Crow—there's a feeling about him. He's different from other creatures. Like us, he *thinks.*"

Crow yielded, but not without misgivings. There was something about snakes that made his pinfeathers prickle.

"Just be careful," Crow suggested. "Don't go getting careless with that reptile."

Four minds considered the point, then rejected it. "We know you'll like him too, Crow. Don't you understand? He's a thinker!"

"I'll judge that when I meet him," Crow said. His craw gnashed and he succumbed to the pang. "I've got to go look for something to eat. You boys haven't seen any fat, juicy grubs lately, have you?"

"No," Dill said, genuinely sorry, "not since the first frost."

"See you again," Crow said, taking wing. The act of flight stirring the biting air chilled him to the marrow.

Partly out of concern for his four identical friends, partly because of a growing curiosity about the rattlesnake, Crow made it a point to drop by the armadillo burrow more often thereafter.

"How's the snake?" Crow asked, by way of greeting.

"Numb," Dill acknowledged. "Sometimes he doesn't even answer us any more."

"What do you suppose makes him that way?" Crow pondered. "Cold-blooded, I mean."

"We asked him that," Dill chorused. "He isn't sure why. He says he has an imperfect three-chambered heart and that might have something to do with it. Anyway, he says he has to go where it's warm in winter and cool in summer, or die."

Crow considered the onus of constantly seeking food, coupled with the burden of finding a pleasant temperature all the while. He decided being a crow had its advantages.

"I never cared much for snakes," Crow admitted. "They go along sticking out their tongues in a most vulgar way."

"He sticks out his tongue to taste the way things smell," Dill said, proud of this inside knowledge.

"Smells with his tongue!" Crow marveled.

"And hears with his belly," Dill laughed. "Snakes have no ears. He feels vibrations instead."

"Red wigglers, Dill!" Crow exclaimed.

"They can't close their eyes, either," Dill added.

"Even when they sleep?"

"Nope. Got little scales over each eye. He lies there sound asleep staring straight at you. Makes your segments shiver just to see it."

"I don't think I'm going to like this creature," Crow confessed. "He has fangs, poison, an odd locomotion, and sleeps with his eyes open!"

"You'll like him," Dill said confidently.

Crow fluffed his feathers to insulate himself, shifting uncomfortably from one black foot to the other.

"He's looking forward to meeting you," Dill said. "We told him all about you—being a thinker and all. He says he's only met one other animal that thinks, besides us."

"Another animal?" Crow said, his eyes sharpening. "What was it?"

"A raccoon," Dill said.

"This is too much!" Crow protested. "Raccoons may be acceptable companions for armadillos, but they have been known to eat crows!"

Distressed, Dill expostulated: "He wouldn't do that, Crow! Not a thinker!"

"I can't be sure of that, Dill."

"You know he wouldn't," Dill insisted. "Would you eat a thinking grub? You might eat grubs all day long, but a *thinking* grub?"

The thought of discovering a thinker in his diet made Crow pace nervously to and fro, the length of his limb above Dill's burrow.

"Answer, Crow!" Dill wailed concertedly. "Would you eat a thinking grub?"

What a horrible prospect! The idea of devouring a tasty grub as it considered its impending fate was so unsettling to Crow that he couldn't reply to Dill's question. After all, what if there were thinking crawdads and thinking caterpillars and thinking— Great grubs! He'd be reduced to a purely vegetable diet. He'd learn to hate other crows for eating his thinking friends! The thought was too terrible to contemplate.

"Well?" Dill demanded. "Would you eat a thinker, Crow?"

"No!" Crow squawked. "But what an odious thought to have to give up grubs if I chanced to meet a thinker among them someday."

"Exactly!" Dill said. "Nor do you need to fear the rattlesnake. He wouldn't eat a thinking crow. For that matter, if there's a thinking raccoon, he wouldn't harm any of us; of that you may be sure."

Somewhat reassured, Crow reserved final judgment nonetheless. "I'll see when I meet them," he yielded. "Until then, I can't prejudge a potential predator."

Satisfied, Dill squinted up at Crow with eight nearsighted eyes and all four heads followed the bird as Crow shoved himself into flight.

"Come again," Dill called.

The relationship evolving between Dill and the rattlesnake disturbed Crow. He spent many hours considering why. Surely his concern was no longer for Dill's collective safety. It was apparent that the rattlesnake intended Dill no harm. The argument about thinkers being above others of their own species was strong. If the rattlesnake was anything like Dill and Crow himself, the idea of harming another thinker was as alien as human ways. So what about the relationship distressed Crow?

Truth comes in many guises. Truth about the faults of others is easily recognized, but an uncomplimentary and demeaning deduction about oneself is as elusive as a gnat. Crow avoided the real reason he was upset about the rattlesnake until at last, being basically honest, and reminding himself that no one untrue to himself can be true to anyone else, Crow analyzed his feelings.

The veil of self-deception lifted and Crow saw himself too clearly. He had done all he could to destroy Dill's blossoming fascination with the rattlesnake. Every comment Crow had offered was designed to plant weeds of doubt, in the hope of choking Dill's respect for the slumbering reptile.

"Snakes are slimy," Crow had observed acidly.

"No, they aren't," Dill had replied. "They're absolutely dry to the touch, Crow. They have no pores, and it's because they can't perspire that they can't cool themselves. It's part of being cold-blooded, don't you see?"

"They're sneaky," Crow insisted.

"Not really," Dill countered mildly. "This rattlesnake is forthright and seems perfectly honorable."

"They're definitely unfriendly," Crow announced. "It's against their nature to be amiable. Otherwise why would they rattle and scare everything away? It's not a cordial overture, Dill. You must admit that."

"He rattles so he won't get stepped on," Dill explained patiently. "He can't shout; snakes have no voice. Being stepped on would not be beneficial to the rattlesnake; and if he had to bite the one who stepped on him, it surely wouldn't be beneficial to him! So the rattle is a safety feature for snake and adversary, both. His poison he uses to secure food, normally. The defensive aspect of the venom is secondary, not intended to be offensive, defensively speaking. And anyway, he can't help rattling."

"Can't help it?" Crow hooted. "Has he no self-control?"

"Now, Crow," Dill chided, very softly, "this isn't like you, to be so narrow-minded. You're condemning the rattlesnake even before you make his acquaintance."

"All right," Crow sulked, "what do you mean he can't help rattling?"

"He says that many snakes shake their tails when they get nervous. The difference is, his tail has segmented scales on it and when he shakes, they make a brr-rring sound. He says he rattles because he has a nervous affliction. He can't help it. Honestly! He shivers like a cattail in high wind, all the time apologizing because his tail is whirring away. He's just a shaky snake, that's all. A *nice* snake, but he's shaky."

"There's something unnerving about a creature that doesn't blink his eyes," Crow said.

"Actually," Dill argued gently, "the snake has an advantage over us, Crow. He burrows through sand, swims in water; nothing gets in his eyes. He never has to blink. That's more efficient than nictitating membranes and outer eyelids, isn't it? And simpler, too. Each eye has a clear scale that's part of his skin. When he sheds, he gets new lenses."

"More efficient than birds?" Crow bristled.

Four unified sighs. The armadillos wondered what had come over the normally genial crow.

The more Dill had defended the rattlesnake, the more

Crow had resented the reptile. Now Crow saw the problem for what it was—he was jealous.

Crow was on the limb over Dill's burrow at the break of dawn the following morning, awaiting Dill's return from their nightly foraging. In due time, he saw the four shielded bodies waddling down the eroded burrows of last season's cornfield, poking their pointed snouts under fallen stalks and rooting for likely edibles.

"I came to beg your pardon," Crow said.

"For what?" Genuine surprise.

"For insulting the rattlesnake."

"But he doesn't know about it," Dill assured Crow.

"Then I shall not apologize to the rattlesnake," Crow explained, "but I owe you four the apology I came to give. I have offended you each and all together. I spent many hours wondering why I acted as I have, and I finally came to understand what made me do it."

"What?" the armadillos asked.

"I was—I *am* jealous."

"Jealous?" The armored heads looked from one to the other of themselves. "What is that?"

The emotion was unknown to Dill.

"Jealous," Crow said, "is when someone resents a loss of attention to himself because a dear associate is interested in a third party."

"Jealous," Dill repeated the word. "Meaning you wanted all the attention for yourself. Undivided attention."

"Yes," Crow confessed, distinctly uncomfortable.

Dill pondered this for a long time, thinking no discernible thoughts. Then their mood changed noticeably.

"That means you are very fond of us!"

"Yes."

"That you want our attention because you like us!"

"Yes," Crow replied.

"Sassafras!" Dill squealed, obviously pleased and resorting to vocal effects.

"Jealousy is not good," Crow counseled. "I will try to suppress it and avoid forming prejudices against the rattlesnake. It is a weakness, jealousy is."

Dill's next thought was soft, tender, very endearing. "Crow?"

"Yes?"

"It wouldn't hurt to be a little jealous now and then—if you wanted to be."

Sensing the importance of this to them, Crow did not disagree.

Dill said, "Being jealous is—if it comes in tiny bunches—a sign of something the rattlesnake told us."

"Really?" Crow was truly impressed that a snake could have considered such a thing before he himself had done so.

"The rattlesnake said that his mother and his brother both left him at his birth. He came from his egg to find a hawk eating his siblings. It seemed to have deeply distressed him. He said, 'There beats no mother's love in a reptile heart.'"

"He said that?" Crow cawed.

"He said he wished that something, somewhere, could love a rattlesnake. He really said that."

Crow was humiliated. No longer did he feel even the faintest tinge of fear for the venomous reptile hibernating in the burrow below. No creature that yearned for love could be all bad—that was a cardinal rule.

"I look forward to meeting your friend the snake," Crow announced.

"Good!" Dill rushed the burrow as a foursome. "We'll get him now!"

60

"No!" Crow halted them. "Let him sleep. The cold above ground might be hazardous to his sluggish blood. I'll see him when warm days come again."

Dill agreed with emanations of sheer joy. It was a good day when any creature expanded his circle of acquaintances to other beings. But it was a fantastic day when such new associations might become friends. Crow and the rattlesnake would be friends, of that Dill was certain.

VII

Moisture just beneath the surface soil had crystallized into frost, making the ground crackle as the crows paced afield. The birds bobbed, walked, bobbed, and again walked a few steps. So meager were their findings, so scarce the edibles, that the search was a mechanical waste of energy. Nonetheless they continued, each individual concentrating on that sparse area he covered.

So intent was their scrutiny, so aching the pangs of hunger, that they had not noticed the waning twilight. Nor did they see the sin perched on a low limb of a far tree. Dusk was an advantage to the nocturnal predator. His large eyes saw them well. The crows saw only what lay beneath their beaks. They had posted no sentries—not one among them was so well fed that he would assume such a position and forgo feeding.

On silent wings and with deadly accuracy came the sin, talons opened wide in the final split second of his plunging attack.

Numbed by cold and hunger, Crow's mother knew nothing

but the task at hand. Separated from the others, she had strayed to one edge of the frozen field. The momentum of the sin's full body weight drove her down, the sin's legs bending under impact, drawing tendons taut and clamping razor-sharp talons like a vise. Crow's mother did not flutter very much.

Had she not been on the ground she might have escaped the attack, or at least survived it. Had it been earlier in the day the other crows might have attacked the sin. But in the ebbing light they became panic-stricken, fearing a similar fate. Without so much as a vocal protest, they fled to the rookery.

His mother had warned Crow of death, constantly stressing the need for vigilance. That she had died for lack of it was unthinkable. For days thereafter, Crow suffered an emptiness not caused by want of food. Alone, he spent hours in solitary search for fuel, thinking of his mother.

Every creature had its positive and negative attributes. Each had a burden unique to its kind. With the cold-blooded rattlesnake, it was the onus of seeking cool areas by summer and warmer regions by winter. With the armadillo it was dull wit and poor eyesight. With Crow it was the unrelenting need of food.

For every negative there was generally a balancing positive. With birds it was the faculty of sight that was most keen. Where Crow learned this he could not say, but he knew it. The eye of a bird was very large compared to those of most other creatures. Often larger than his brain, the bird's eye was almost immovable in its bony socket.

With eyes placed well forward, giving them an overlapping field of vision, the predatory birds enjoyed excellent depth perception. The eagle could spy a stock-still hare from a height of half a mile. The hawk easily caught the flick of a squirrel's busy tail several hundred yards distant.

Other birds, such as the sparrow, with eyes placed well back on the sides of its head, could see fore and aft with equal ease, each eye independently alert. And what eyes! Most birds could peer intently at a tiny object an inch from the beak and shift in a fraction of a second to acute perception at long distance. So it was with the duck; with eyes placed back and higher than most birds, the waterfowl could literally see full circle at once. The sin, on the other hand, had to turn his entire head to see any way but straight forward.

The ability did not necessarily mean the bird *saw*, though. Through carelessness, Crow's mother had become prey.

Crow was forced to an angry conclusion: a talent in disuse, even momentarily, was a weakness. Having the ability to do something and not doing it might be worse than not having it. Crow decided he had so many negatives—poor detection of odor and sense of touch being the most notable—that he could hardly afford a careless lapse of his positives.

His mother's death made Crow vow to keep himself alert, utilize his strengths, and overcome his weaknesses as best he could. Therein might he find long life. Otherwise, death at an early age was a certainty.

The increasing paucity of food exposed an ugly element in the rookery. Each bird fended for himself. Their crucial sentry system had deteriorated. The flock bickered constantly. A tasty tidbit was often wasted as several crows fought over it, reducing the edible to shreds benefiting none.

Disgusted, Crow withdrew from the rookery, seeking refuge and inner sanity by himself. Mindful of the danger of being alone, still he preferred no company to that of the flock.

For several days he changed roosting places by chance more than design. Now he perched on a denuded cypress, an icy drizzle permeating his plumage. His craw was empty and poor hunting for three days had left him depleted. Weakly he shook himself in a futile effort to dispel the steadily deepening chill in his body. Any flight took concerted effort, leaving him exhausted. His muscles ached constantly.

The world was a depressing expanse of grey skies, unrelenting rainfall, and biting temperatures. Would the sun never shine again? Was this something all living things must endure? Surely there was someplace where the sky was clear and the sun warmed the sod.

"I say, bird!"

So low were Crow's spirits, so great his discomfort, he did not move.

"I say, bird there—this is my tree!"

Crow extended his head only slightly from between his hunched wings. He blinked his eyes and stared along the limb upon which he perched. Where the bough junctured with the trunk, a hole was filled with the masked face of a young raccoon.

"You must be the rattlesnake's friend," Crow said, with no cheer in his voice.

"Rattlesnake? Why, yes, I suppose I am that." The raccoon had pushed his head out, but as rain flecked his whiskers he again withdrew to the dry comfort of his den.

"How is Adam?" the raccoon inquired. "I haven't seen him for some time."

"He's underground," Crow explained. "Sharing the burrow with an armadillo friend of mine. *Four* armadillo friends."

"Seems I do recall him saying something about having to do that," the raccoon noted. "Part of being a serpent, I understand. He's a nice snake, as snakes go."

"Listen," Crow asked, "you wouldn't happen to have a juicy grub in there, would you?"

"No, I'm sorry. I haven't seen a grub since the first frost." Crow attempted to ruffle his feathers and they shifted sluggishly. He shivered involuntarily.

"I think I'm dying," Crow said, matter-of-factly.

"What's the problem?" the raccoon asked.

"I'm starving. I'm cold. I'm wet. I'm unhappy."

"You might die of starvation or exposure," the raccoon laughed, "but nothing dies from being unhappy."

Crow peered at the masked face through nictitating membranes. "Do you know that, except for the armadillos, the rattlesnake, and me, you are only the fourth creature I've met that thinks—communicates?"

The raccoon pondered that a moment, then announced, "In which case, as one of a rare type, I guess I'd better not let you starve to death."

The raccoon disappeared and Crow heard the scraping of toenails as the furry animal lowered himself through the hollowed trunk of the cypress. Emerging at ground level, the raccoon beckoned to Crow and walked off. The miserable bird made short, hopping flights from point to point, keeping up with the waddling form below.

"There!" the raccoon pronounced, halting at the edge of a creek.

"There where?" Crow questioned.

"There right there," Raccoon said. "I had a bit of fortune in my angling this past evening and there's the remains of my catch. You do eat fish, do you not?"

Crow almost dropped to the ground, but an instinctive caution halted him.

"You won't attack me?" Crow asked.

"Chiggers, no! Why would I do that?"

"I don't know," Crow ventured. He knew he faced the real

possibility that tomorrow he would be too weak to hunt. Still, he couldn't bring himself to go below.

"If it will make you feel easier," Raccoon said, "I'll go off some distance."

Crow subdued his fears. "No," he said. "That would be rude and ungrateful of me."

Crow alit not three feet from the raccoon and the two creatures stared at one another openly.

"I never saw a bird this close before," Raccoon said. Then, to reassure Crow: "Please—eat!"

Crow attacked the carrion in utter abandon. Oblivious to the raccoon, the land around him, the sky overhead, he gorged himself. With each swallow, strength returned in tiny waves. He ate until his craw stuck out below his beak in a most comforting discomfort.

"You're looking better already," Raccoon said.

"And feeling better," Crow stated. "I thank you."

"Now, if you don't mind," Raccoon said, "I'm getting soaked to the skin and my feet are cold. I'm going back to my hole in the tree."

"Of course," Crow acknowledged, realizing the raccoon had been standing by out of courtesy.

"You're welcome to stay," the raccoon said, departing. "There's a holly tree not far from here that affords good shelter. Nothing frequents that tree. There's a scuppernong vine in it that bears a good crop, I'm told. I keep going by to see, but so far nothing has happened."

"Thanks!" Crow cawed. Then as the last wobbling glimpse of the raccoon's posterior vanished beneath a palmetto frond, Crow said again, softly: "Thanks!"

The masked animal's reply came to Crow's mind. "You're welcome. We'll spend some time together tomorrow."

67

Crow took lodging in the holly tree beneath sharp, pointed leaves. He stroked his bill on both sides against a twig, scraping away excess pieces of fish. His craw filled, body heat rising, he spent the balance of the daylight hours combing his feathers. The barbed filaments rezippered, forming an air- and water-tight bond. Taking oil from the nub on his tail, Crow applied the fluid to his plumage, restoring its water-repellent qualities. His will to exist rose with each passing minute and the food, combined with the grooming, returned a bearing of pride to the bird.

"Dill was right," Crow decided. "Nothing that thinks is going to hurt another thinker."

He ruffled his feathers, thereby insulating himself. He had been so hungry! So weak and emaciated.

Crow jerked erect as he remembered the abandon with which he had fallen upon the meal. He could easily have been attacked! That's how his mother had died. She'd been hungry—uncaring, perhaps—and she had fallen prey to the sin. Crow reexamined his earlier thoughts about her death. He remembered his resolve never to be lax in vigilance. After his experience of today, Crow amended his earlier condemnations of the reckless ones.

A talent in disuse was a weakness. True.

Another, more mature observation: From a position of strength, it is easy to criticize the weak.

The raccoon called himself "Lotor," and he was not yet one season old. Despite his youth he was wily, industrious, and intelligent. Doing his prowling mostly at the edges of day and night, the raccoon chattered constantly as Crow sat watching on a limb somewhere above.

"Chiggers, this water's cold!" Lotor said, pumping his forepaws up and down, feeling with five tiny fingers for a hidden crustacean. "But," he added pleasantly, "the mud feels good between my toes."

"Why do you bathe everything before you eat it?" Crow inquired.

"My saliva glands are not well-developed," Lotor explained. "Dunking food in water to moisten it helps me swallow. I'm not really washing the food."

"I have no saliva either," Crow remarked. "I don't dunk food."

"No," Lotor agreed, "but you don't chew it, nor do you have to make a contraction of the gullet to swallow. With birds, food goes down in gulps. That's why you throw back your head to make water go down your throat."

Amazed at this insight into his own body by an alien, Crow said, "That's very astute, Lotor."

"Want a crawdad?" Lotor offered, first biting the creature, then delivering it to the sandy bank of the creek.

"Thanks!" Crow strolled beside the raccoon.

"Something I've noticed," Lotor observed, talking incessantly as he probed the creek bottom. "Snakes are reviled by most other animals. Birds enjoy a certain respect, particularly from humans."

"Not all birds," Crow said ruefully.

"Most birds," Lotor amended.

"So?"

"It just seems ironic, that's all," Lotor chirped, his tone signaling the find of another crawdad.

"Ironic how?" Crow asked.

"Birds are the snakes' relatives, descended from them."

Shocked, Crow stared at the raccoon.

"Does that disturb you?" Lotor asked.

"I—well—yes, actually, though I don't know why," Crow confessed. "Where did you get such an idea?"

"I entranced myself one very cold day and it came to me when I was thinking about Adam, the rattlesnake."

"Entranced yourself?" Crow questioned.

"Sure, don't you ever do that?"

"What is it?"

"Meditation, sort of," Lotor chattered loquaciously. "Just put the brain in limbo. You can learn to direct it, seeking whatever information you want, but that takes practice."

"But this is unbelievable," Crow whispered. "I've never done it, and yet somehow I know how it feels."

"I'll teach you sometime. I showed Adam how to do it. Very smart snake. He caught on right away."

Suddenly Lotor thrashed wildly, whirling in circles as though he'd gone mad. "Come on, you!" Lotor shrieked. "Gotcha! Sweet scuppernongs! Oh no, oh no you don't! Come here!"

Thrusting his entire head below water, Lotor emerged with a tremendous fish flopping between his jaws. So large was the prey that each flip snapped Lotor's head this way and that.

"We eat, Crow!" Lotor exulted.

Placing the fish a safe distance from the water, Lotor commenced to shred flesh. He said, "I named the rattlesnake Adam. Took it from *Adamanteus.* Humans call his type *Crotalus adamanteus.* Crotalus means 'a large rattle,' and adamanteus means 'unyielding.' So I named him 'Adam,' which has a certain significance, if you know what I mean."

Crow did not know what Lotor meant, but after having listened to the raccoon talking nonstop all day, he didn't particularly want to open a freshet of explanations.

"Umm," Crow said, speaking of the fish, "delicious!"

"I think catching him gave me a crick in my neck," Lotor commented, still shredding the meat, mostly for Crow's benefit.

70

VIII

Stalactites of frozen water tipped each thorny leaf of the holly, and a cutting breeze pierced Crow's body. During the night his feet had frozen to the limb, and for a panic-stricken instant he thought himself ensnared forever. Then he tore loose. Repositioning himself, he hunched his wings, pulling in his neck as far as possible. An incessant mist and the low temperature had sheathed the woodlands in ice.

Had it not been for Lotor during this dismal period, Crow would surely have died. The raccoon foraged for both of them. His charity came with a small price: Lotor talked constantly, a verbal barrage that assaulted the senses. Never ceasing, the raccoon tendered an opinion on virtually everything under the sun, expounding endlessly on any topic to strike his fancy. Inundated with words, Crow soon discovered that it was not conversation Lotor sought, which is a give-and-take between two minds. What Lotor required was a listener. Any debate involved was between Lotor and himself. Lotor sometimes talked himself out of one firm conviction and into a complete about-face on the same issue.

Unfortunately, Lotor's interminable dissertations did not engender a desire to listen closely to anything he said. Drowned in a torrent of words, Crow often found himself oblivious to a specific point Lotor had made.

Gritting his teeth, up to his chin whiskers in frigid water, Lotor pumped his forepaws, fishing and talking.

"Chiggers!" Lotor snorted suddenly. "That was a big one and I let him get away."

"Fish?" Crow inquired.

"Crawdad. Ah! Got the bugger this time."

Crunch. Lotor decapitated the crayfish and gave the rest to Crow.

"So humans have splendid words, but still they don't communicate as well as we do," Lotor said.

Whatever Lotor had said heretofore was lost, and now Crow's interest was piqued.

"Why do you say that, Lotor?"

"Because of what I just said!" Lotor said, turning to gaze at Crow. "Aren't you listening?"

Before Crow could admit his mind had wandered, Lotor spun in the creek and began thrashing water. "Sweet scuppernongs, Crow! Another one. Sweet scuppernongs! I've found a bed of the little buggers!"

In a frenzy, Lotor fished one crawdad after another up from the water, biting the chilled edibles to render them all the more immobile, then tossing them out to Crow on the bank.

"Look at the size of that one, would you!" Lotor exulted. "I'll eat the head."

"I'm stuffed," Crow said.

"Good, aren't they?" Lotor chirped, taking this as a cue that he could devour any more crawdads he found. He was finding plenty of them, too, lying dormant in the mud.

"How did you learn about humans?" Crow asked.

"Entrancement," Lotor replied. "It's the access to all knowledge, remember?"

In the weeks that followed, Crow brought the conversation around to entrancement again and again. As he and Lotor ranged the frozen swampland searching for food, Lotor displayed an amazing understanding of many things—all the while confessing that he had never been beyond the acreage he called home.

"You can learn anything you want," Lotor tutored. "It's easy, once you master the techniques."

Each time the subject of entrancement arose, Crow tried to absorb the mood required and learn the mental exercises he must accomplish. He had nagging doubts that he would ever attain full entrancement. For one thing, Lotor in a hollow tree or Adam the rattlesnake in a deep burrow might be able to abandon their bodies with relative safety, but it was not that simple for Crow. In his absence, what would befall his body perching in a tree? He might return to find himself in remnants, being devoured by some predator.

Nonetheless, the idea was utterly intriguing. Crow considered it, debated, and finally made a halfhearted attempt at it, but became frightened at the last moment and aroused himself with a squawk.

When full entrancement finally came, it came by accident. For three days the Gulf area had been beset with record low temperatures. The rare freeze, coupled with the normal high humidity of the region, made every stir of wind an agony that penetrated Lotor's fur and Crow's feathers, rendering them incapable of normal movement.

Here and there, lifeless bodies of birds and mammals,

victims of starvation and exposure, littered the landscape.

There was no escape from the elements. Crow's outer feathers were glazed with moisture which had crystallized into an icy jacket. He wished fervently that the sun would shine, that the trees would green anew, and that he could return to the rookery and find the flock happy, contented, and well fed. If this could not be so this instant, at least could he be somewhere else?

Suddenly a strange aroma filled the air, a pleasant odor that he soon identified as dates on a palm tree. The sun was a fiery orb overhead and a tepid breeze blew in from the ocean. Waves curled and beached—and the sand! Not the white bleached sands of the Alabama Gulf Coast which he knew so well; this sand was coarse, yellow, beautiful!

The cries of a dozen species of birds came to his ears, and not a single crow among them. A pelican soared toward Crow on fixed wings, borne across the waters atop a pillow of air holding the big bird just above the tips of the waves. When it appeared the pelican would bump him, Crow opened his mouth to cry out a warning and assert himself. The voice he uttered stunned him.

Crow cocked his head and looked down at his own breast. *Brown?* His feet were barely visible beneath a huge breast and a sac under his bill! His feet were webbed!

"What am I?" he screamed.

His panic catapulted Crow back to the holly tree, and immediately the throb of nearly frozen appendages made his muscles ache.

"What happened?" he asked himself.

"Was it unpleasant?" Lotor's voice.

"No, Lotor."

"Then do it again, Crow."

"I'm afraid," Crow whispered.

"Don't be afraid," Lotor assured him, gently. "Go and learn. Nothing can hurt you where you're going. You can always come back here. Go, Crow. Go again. Learn. Enjoy."

Crow felt his inner eyelids closing and he let himself relax.

"Think no bad thoughts," Lotor's voice murmured comfortingly. "Let the mind idle. Feel no pain, no wind. Feel nothing. Let the mind go where it may, do as it wishes. Peregrinate, Crow. Let the mind wander untethered."

Crow ebbed over more easily this time. With a final stab of fear for his physical safety, Crow paused.

"I'll look after you, Crow," Lotor whispered.

Crow was gone.

For five days, Lotor came to the holly tree and sat on the limb with Crow, gazing at the apparently frozen bird. But Crow was not dead. Lotor knew that. From the iced, feathered figure came a distinct hum.

Lotor spent his evenings alone, but far lonelier than ever before in his life. Until now, he had never felt a particular need for companionship. He had never thought the word "lonely" before.

Disgusted, cold and wet, his hairs turning to frozen spikes as he waddled toward the holly tree each morning, Lotor grunted and snorted, chattering almost as much to himself as he did when he had an audience to heed him.

"Should never have taught him entrancement," Lotor muttered. "Been gone far too long. Most likely he'll leave his body here to starve. I can't force-feed a frozen crow!"

Lotor labored up the ice-sheathed trunk of the tree. Attaining the bough that was Crow's roost, the raccoon positioned himself very near to the statuelike figure, using his body heat to warm the bird.

"Where do you suppose he's gone?" Lotor fussed, shifting to warm Crow's other side. "Leaves me sitting here with the body while he takes off, probably basking on a tropical island nibbling scuppernongs."

Lotor touched one of Crow's feet and the temperature of that appendage alarmed the raccoon.

"Come back, Crow," Lotor whispered.

The raccoon hovered over the inert bird, warming and shielding, chirping to himself and imploring, "Come back, Crow."

It was the sound of dripping water that Crow first heard as he returned. Cascading droplets from the uppermost leaves of the holly gathered weight, teetered at the tips of spiked leaves, and fell to the bowers below. Ultimately each succeeding drop joined others, and from the lower reaches of the tree the earth was pelted by a shower of melting ice.

Crow's eye fixed on a single drop, a gem radiating reflected shards of a rising sun. His roost was moist, the air warmer than when he slipped away entranced. Shifting his vision, he focused on Lotor curled in a crotch of the holly.

"Hello, Crow."

"Hello, Lotor."

"You were gone too long, Crow," Lotor said testily.

"I'm sorry."

The raccoon extended his legs in a distinctly feline gesture, stretching muscle kinks, toes separated, quivering with the effort. Then relaxing, Lotor crawled out of the crook in the tree, grabbed the limb with his front claws, and pulled in such a way that his spine was protracted.

"I worried you, Lotor," Crow realized. "I'm sorry."

Lotor bathed his masked face, briskly brushing the lengthy whiskers, eyes squinted. "It's all right," he said, but his mood indicated it wasn't.

"You've been watching over me?" Crow inquired gently.

"I couldn't very well leave you to freeze or be eaten."

"Was there any danger of that?" Crow asked.

"Of being frozen, certainly! I'm glad I don't have to spend my nights perched on a roost."

Crow ached from keeping his toes clamped so long. He flapped his wings a few times, keeping himself anchored all the while.

"I'm hungry," Crow confessed.

"No doubt," Lotor commented coolly. "We'll see what we can find."

"The sun's shining!" Crow said, as though only now aware of it. Lotor grunted.

At first in silence, then with increasing animation, Lotor poked under shrubs and peeked beneath an occasional stone, his loquacious nature reasserting itself.

"Where'd you go?" Lotor called up to Crow.

"To find myself."

"Well, did you?"

"I think so."

"Did you like what you found?" Lotor questioned, sticking a toe down a hole and withdrawing it to peer at nothing. The hole was empty.

"I didn't like or dislike it," Crow said. "It's not a matter of like or dislike. I found me, for better or worse. Some of it I don't understand."

"Like what?" Lotor asked, pausing to look up at Crow on a low limb overhead.

"I think I went back to the egg before I was hatched," Crow said. "I felt the egg tumble. I saw sunshine through the shell. But I had the strange feeling it wasn't really me there at all. It didn't make sense."

"Must've been a bad trip," Lotor mused.

"It wasn't unpleasant," Crow amended. "Except parts of it. I saw a lot of dead animals and birds everywhere I went."

"Dead from what?" Lotor asked, resuming his trek toward their favorite stream.

"I don't know. I didn't stop to find out. It was just a dream."

"A dream?" Lotor snapped, wheeling to face Crow. "Is that what you think it was?"

"It felt like a dream, I mean."

"You may be sure it was not a dream, friend Crow," Lotor said emphatically. Then, in a softer tone: "Did you learn anything?"

"I think so, Lotor."

"Well?" Lotor asked impatiently. "What did you learn?"

"I've lived before. Before this lifetime, I mean."

"You must be getting delirious, Crow. Must be hunger."

"I was once a very old bird named 'Mayor,' and somehow I was hatched anew."

"Get some food in your craw and you'll feel better," Lotor said, hurrying his pace a bit.

"I was reborn—rehatched. Somewhere in the egg, I lost my memory of the other lifetime."

"A little food will do it," Lotor said, his tone insistent.

"I want to go back and try to find out," Crow said.

"Crawdad, earthworm, anything," Lotor mumbled, his paws moving rapidly as he stirred some leaves.

Crow dropped to a bush near the busy raccoon.

"It's true, Lotor," he said with intensity.

"Ah, a worm! Here, Crow, eat this."

Crow settled beside Lotor and accepted the morsel.

"Another one, Crow, here, eat it. The moisture is driving them out of the soil. Wiggly little thing, isn't it?"

The two hunted as Crow listened and Lotor unleashed a flood of observations.

"Worms have no front or back as such, so far as I can determine. You want to start with the head, right? It's more merciful. But you can never be sure which end is which. Did you ever think about that, Crow?"

"Simply delicious," Crow sighed.

"It's nearly impossible to chomp both ends at the same time," Lotor continued. "I've tried. They won't stand still for it."

"I would've died this winter if it hadn't been for you, Lotor," Crow said.

The unexpected seriousness halted Lotor verbally and physically.

"I doubt it, Crow."

"I would've died and you know it, Lotor. I thank you."

"Forget it," Lotor said, the just recognition of his benevolence warming him.

"A grub!" Crow squawked. He seized the pudgy insect and was about to swallow it when he detected Lotor's response to the find.

"Here," Crow said, placing it before the raccoon.

"Oh, I couldn't."

"Please. It's yours."

The raccoon stared at the choice morsel, then began to fondle it between both front feet.

"It even feels good," Lotor said softly. Then, when he could stand the anticipation no longer, he ate it, chewing it thoroughly as raccoons do.

It was one of the pleasantest days of Crow's life. The raccoon and Crow sated themselves on emerging larvae. They laughed at one another, chasing food their bodies could no longer contain.

Finally, gorged, they withdrew to Lotor's cypress den and there wiled away the afternoon at Lotor's favorite pastime— talking.

IX

In a way that can only happen in southern coastal areas, spring was nowhere to be seen one day and everywhere the next. Tiny slivers of green pushed out of winter-tight buds. The oaks were last to accept the new season finery, having allowed most other hardwood trees to clothe themselves first. Flying high and alone, Crow saw the emergence of entire fields, a day ago dull and lifeless, today a wave of green.

With a change in clime, thousands of avian migrants appeared as though from the thawing earth itself. Arriving at night or on the first rays of morning sunlight, their appearance was the final proof that winter was done.

Moving from the marshy habitat that had been their cold-weather abode, Lotor and Crow took advantage of the changing situation. From lowland to high ground they went. Lotor, now easily fed, was most pleasant immediately before sunrise and shortly before dusk.

As the nocturnal raccoon slept away his days, Crow foraged

alone, his strength and energy reserve mounting. For the first time in weeks he went to the burrow of the armadillo brothers.

"What say, Crow!" one of the armadillos greeted him. "H-h-how goes it?"

"Doing fine," Crow replied. "And you?"

"V-v-very good. Wait a m-m-minute, let me get my brothers." Into the burrow disappeared the armored one and momentarily all four shielded faces emerged.

"Where've you been?" Dill inquired, the full assembly of their collective brains eliminating the hesitation in speech.

"I met Lotor, the raccoon that's the rattlesnake's friend," Crow said. "He saved my life. I was starving and he fed me."

"You see!" Dill said. "We said that no thinker would ever harm another thinker."

"Yes, you did."

"Didn't we?" Dill insisted.

"Yes, you did, Dill."

"We were right, weren't we?"

"Yes, you were," Crow acknowledged. "Is the rattlesnake still here?"

"Oh, yes. The turtle's gone. Good riddance, too. Never once said thanks for the hospitality. Got up one day and stalked off, like it was the divine right of a gopher turtle to tie up a burrow for the winter."

"Why doesn't the rattlesnake come out?" Crow asked.

"Oh, he has. He does. He began to stir shortly after the gopher turtle left. Comes out every morning to soak up sunshine, and then back into the burrow at night. One day he went off and got something to eat. He's down below now, taking it easy."

Crow fidgeted uncomfortably for a few minutes, hoping Dill would offer to fetch the reptile. When that idea had not occurred to them in a reasonable period, Crow suggested, "Maybe I could meet him now?"

"Oh, for—sure! Hang on there, Crow."

One of the quadruplets went below. They waited and waited and waited. Finally, out of the burrow came the armadillo, who turned and faced the hole expectantly.

The first thing Crow saw was a forked tongue lapping the air. The next to appear was the reptile, the projecting scales over his eyes giving him a permanently unfriendly glare. The triangular head paused at the mouth of the burrow, tongue testing the air.

"The name's Crow," Crow said.

Zip! The snake was gone.

"Hello there, Adam!" Crow called. "I'm a friend of Lotor's."

"Lotor?" the rattlesnake's thought returned to Crow.

"He speaks highly of you. I'd like to make your acquaintance."

Once more the tentatively probing tongue emerged, then the scaled head and unblinking eyes. Finally, gathering every iota of his courage, Adam came forth. It was a false start. When Crow dropped down from the tree, the rattlesnake dived back into his hole, tail whirring.

"He's nervous," Dill explained.

"Very nervous," Crow agreed. "Hello, Adam, it was just me, Crow."

"Please forgive me," Adam said, still not to be seen. "Hush, tail! I'm very sorry, Crow. I can't help it. Excuse my vibrations."

"Don't worry about it," Crow said, with more assurance than he actually felt. The rattling tail did not calm the bird. It was a frightening alarm, regardless of Adam's true intentions.

"Shush, tail, now *shush!*" Adam demanded.

"Do come out now, Adam," Dill urged.

"I wish I could, I really wish it," the snake said, his thought tremulous. "I want to, you know that. I really want to do it. Now tail, I want you to *cease* that!"

Patiently, Crow waited.

At last, with obvious trepidation despite his positively menacing expression, Adam came into view. Tongue flicking, head poised as though listening for a far sound, the earless creature gazed at Crow.

"I'm afraid, you know," Adam said.

"Yes, I know," Crow said, "but you needn't fear me."

"I must apologize for my tail," Adam blurted. "It has no propriety and very little to do with my friendliness. I sometimes wish I could bang it on a rock and break those rattles off. I do hope you aren't offended."

"Not in the least," Crow said. That was true, but his heart was still hammering, and it was all Crow could do to muster a warm tone after such a cold-blooded welcome.

"How is Lotor?" Adam asked.

"Fat as can be," Crow said. "We've been stuffing ourselves with everything imaginable. Winter was a tough period. I hope they aren't all like that."

"I'm glad I'm cold-blooded," Adam said. "Being chilled and still having to seek food would be most unpleasant. My metabolism is very slow when I get cold."

Crow cawed aloud, laughing. "Here I felt sorry for you because you couldn't move around in winter! I guess being cold-blooded has an advantage after all."

"Oh, decidedly so! Some reptiles can go six months without water and a year or more without food. Being cold-blooded is a distinct advantage when meals are far apart and it's cold."

"I would say," Dill said, "that we are all happy to be what we are."

"Well put," Crow acknowledged.

"Is Lotor coming over?" Adam inquired, now coiling into loops, his head atop the heap of his own body.

"I would assume he will," Crow said. "But he's asleep at the moment. He prefers night foraging."

"Actually, so do I," Adam said. An undulating ripple traversed the serpent's body in what was, so far as Crow could determine, a reptilian mannerism akin to Crow's smoothing his feathers.

"Say, Crow," Dill interjected, "what's happening to all the birds?"

"What do you mean?"

"We're finding them all over the place," Dill said. "Dead."

"What killed them?"

"No idea. They're just dead, that's all."

"What kind of birds?" Crow asked.

"Mockers, robins, thrushes . . ." Dill hesitated. "Crows."

"I haven't been to the rookery in a long while," Crow said, his tone low.

"Maybe it's natural this time of year," Dill suggested.

"Maybe," Crow said. Abruptly he addressed the rattlesnake. "I have to go, Adam. I'm sorry."

"I understand."

Crow's flurry of wings made the rattler jerk back, head lifted, tail whirring. "Oh, for— Stop it, tail!"

Crow rose over the field, an urgency in his downbeats, rushing where he should have gone first, perhaps: to the rookery.

"Here now!" he heard Adam's self-admonishment. "Would you cut that out. Dill, grab that thing and see if you can stop it."

"No thanks!" Dill chorused.

*　　*　　*

85

Crows are by nature low-flying birds, avoiding ostentatious altitudes. Elevation brings unnecessary exposure and the perils thereof. Even en masse they prefer skimming treetops as opposed to high-level migrations. Thus Crow had never attempted to ascend beyond an altitude required to move from one point to another.

But when he found the rookery deserted, Crow began to climb. Higher and higher he flew, keenly alert to the diminishing topography, looking for fellow crows. A hazy miasma fell away below him as he attained eminence. The temperature dropped noticeably. Utilizing his sight with perception he did not know he possessed, he searched the patchwork-quilt landscape. Attuned to any movement, he watched for ebony flecks that might be his kin.

He met his first cumulus. Entering the billow of moisture, he was immediately buffeted by thermal currents. With heady exhilaration he was cast hundreds of feet higher in a few seconds. His feathers were ruffled from the rising air and, in flight, he had to flex muscles to realign the primary quills.

Puffs of pure white vapors fell away below him, and Crow lost some of the advantage of altitude as sections of land were obscured by clouds. Suddenly he was battling a relentless flow of air, and even his most powerful wing beats did not carry him forward. Since direction was not a consideration, he turned and, with the wind now at his tail, he was transported at unbelievable speed. Far below, like a puddle, Mobile Bay twined away to the north and expanded into the Gulf to the south.

Closing his wings, Crow dropped out of the current of wind and wheeled to go back. In the space of a few moments he had been carried miles! He saw the earth in a perspective he had never known existed. Entire cities were mere specks.

But this was not finding the flock. Crow dropped lower still, forcing himself to resume the search and resolving to come test the heavens another time. Did the high altitude river of wind blow constantly? How far did it flow? Did it change direction? Quelling his curiosity, reminding himself of the rookery, his will to find his community regained, Crow flew homeward. Down, down into the clouds again he fell, and below; his wings splayed like spread fingers, deliberately slipping.

Crow waited at the rookery for the evening return of the flock. As was the custom with gregarious crows, they came in clusters, silently approaching the roosting area. Once the "all clear" was sounded, they burst into jabbering, argumentative exchanges. Brief disputes erupted when thieves were caught honing their talents or a favorite perch was contested.

Crow quietly observed their assembly, noting acquaintances, friends, and elders. There were a few strangers who had migrated in during the winter. But the total flock was half what it had been last spring. Ravaged by disease, accident, and winter famine, the community had altered considerably. This could be expected. It was nature's way of equalizing life with the counterbalances of food and territorial requirements.

The flock went about the business of living as though nothing were amiss. Death from the hazards of daily living received only fleeting remorse from survivors. Mortalities of nature were a debt which all living things must ultimately pay.

A natural death leaves little residue. The weak and ill become prey, and the victims are immediately devoured. Demise from old age was rare, but when it occurred the elderly sought solitude in their final hours, away from the flock. In the natural cycle of supply and demand, a body was fodder to possums, rodents, and insects so that no death was truly a waste of life.

It took Crow several days to determine what had been worrying him about the scene.

Of course! It was the balance of the deaths, the ages of the dead that was unnatural.

The dead were not inexperienced and unwary fledglings. The greatest loss had befallen mature crows—and that was not normal.

The loss of an elder always affects a rookery. The elder represents that reservoir of experience and counseling which tempers a community. The older he is, the greater his learning and knowledge. Long life was evidence of an individual's intelligence, guile, and fortitude. Only fledglings and fools ignored such ancients.

The wave of death had upset the social balance of the rookery—and this was what made it contrary to the cycle of life.

"Why have so many older crows died?" Crow asked a five-year-old member of the community.

"It was a harsh winter," came the reply.

"But so many of those who died were mature crows," Crow insisted.

"Nothing unusual about that," a young elder retorted.

"Nothing unusual at all," another responded, joining the conversation. "Plenty of creatures didn't make it. Not only crows—all kinds of animals."

Crow flew with the flock in quest of food, settling once more into the routine of rookery living.

"We thought you were one of the dead," a fellow yearling commented.

"No," Crow said. "I spent the winter alone."

"Very hazardous," a young elder stated. "It's always best to remain with the flock. Numerically, your chances for survival are greatest within the rookery."

Studying the community, Crow was disturbed to see how the adversity of winter had affected them.

"Elder," Crow questioned one of the oldest of the young elders, "shouldn't we reestablish the sentry system?"

"Do you think me stupid?" the young elder snapped. "Where have you been? When we tried to get these fledglings to stand sentry duty, they were totally unreliable! The fools think their own craws are more important than the common good."

"Surely they see the need for sentries," Crow implored.

"A few years ago," the young elder seethed, "a lax sentry would have been tried and punished. Nowadays they scream bloody murder if we accuse one of inattention. We couldn't get a court to convict them even in the face of overwhelming evidence."

The problem was, the elders were not yet old enough to command the respect necessary to deliver judgments.

"The society will fail," Crow warned, "if order is not reestablished, elder."

"Go away," the elder fumed. "I have a skull full of problems and I'm not feeling well."

"Perhaps a council should be called," Crow suggested.

"Go away, yearling!" the elder demanded. "Leave government to the older crows."

Everywhere about him, Crow saw yearlings break the law with impunity. Several young crows assaulted an older female and robbed her of food. This should have earned the interlopers a severe community whipping. The flock gave it only passing notice and did nothing.

The rookery needed an elder who commanded respect. Crow went to seek the young elder he had approached a few days before. What he found struck Crow with panic.

"That elder died," he was told.

"Died?" Crow cried. "He was a young elder!"

"Nevertheless, he's dead."

"From what?" Crow questioned.

"Who knows?" another crow sighed. "It was a harsh winter."

X

Crow circled over Dill's burrow twice before settling on a limb above the armadillo home. Lying to one side, basking in the sun, was Adam the rattlesnake.

"Good morning, Adam," Crow said.

The rattlesnake responded with a physical jerk, his thoughts invaded by Crow's greeting.

"Good morning, Crow."

"Where is Dill?"

"Sleeping, I think," Adam replied, his nervousness subsiding. "Come down and join me, Crow."

This Crow did, landing a few feet from the glowering reptile.

"It's a pleasant day," Crow observed.

"Indeed, most pleasant," Adam said. "What brings you this way, Crow?"

Crow related the events of the past few days. He was not interrupted as he told about the dead crows and the untimely and mysterious death of the young elder which had occurred only yesterday.

"I've noticed many dead things," Adam said. "It's been a boon to creatures which feed on carrion. As for myself, I'm having difficulty finding meals. Snakes prefer live foods. We don't eat vegetation or dead things, you know."

It crossed Crow's mind that *he* was alive, and that many snakes eat birds and eggs.

Adam hastened to add, "I prefer rodents and rabbits, Crow. And of course it would never do to eat a fellow thinker."

"Thank you, Adam."

"I shouldn't want you to think I gaze upon you as a delectable, Crow."

"Thank you, Adam."

"That would not enter my mind." Then after a pause, Adam felt it necessary to add, "Unfortunately, this is not so with all rattlesnakes."

"I realize that, Adam."

"You should not assume that other rattlers are so selective," Adam commented.

"I assumed no such thing, Adam."

"A word to the wise, that's all," Adam concluded. "Did you want to wake the armadillos?"

"No. I was only looking for someone with whom to discuss all this," Crow stated. "I tried to find Lotor and couldn't."

"He sleeps by day, as you know," Adam said.

"All the deaths are really worrying me," Crow said.

"Dying is a natural part of living," Adam remarked.

"Natural death is," Crow said. "These deaths aren't natural. I flew down to the bay yesterday afternoon, and waterfowl are experiencing the same thing. Mature birds are dying while younger ones seem immune. Everyone is blaming it on winter, but that doesn't make sense now. Winter is past and food supplies are increasing."

"At least it's a good year for the carrion-eaters," Adam said philosophically. The rattlesnake was listening, but not truly interested in the subject.

"I found pigeons dead on the ledges of city buildings," Crow continued. "Sparrows are lying beside barn walls. And not only birds. There were two armadillos which appeared to be perfectly all right, but they, too, were dead. One raccoon, but he may have died of old age. I don't really judge the age of other creatures too well."

"Any snakes?" Adam asked.

"Only one or two on the highways, the usual thing."

"Would that suggest to you that the others are dying because they're warm-blooded?" Adam inquired.

"Possibly."

"Reptiles are immune to certain diseases which affect warm-blooded creatures."

"That may be a clue," Crow said.

"Perhaps the disease is transmitted through carrion. If that is so, Dill won't live long. Carrion is about all the armadillos are consuming these days. They say there's no point wasting energy when so much food is lying around everywhere."

"It probably doesn't matter," Crow stated. "Creatures that don't eat carrion are dying, too."

Adam's tongue flickered through his cleft upper lip. "It must be a virus," he concluded.

"Then why are the younger animals immune?" Crow asked.

"I don't know," Adam sighed. "Crow, will you excuse me? We have depressed me. I'm going below."

Crow returned to the rookery, distraught by all he had seen.

He vowed to stir the elders to action. If nothing else, they could at least issue a warning to the youths still blinded by inexperience.

Crow asked the oldest elder, "Elder, have you considered why there are so many deaths suddenly among the mature crows?"

"I am still assessing the situation," the elder said. "There will be a statement in the near future."

There was the problem with young elders. They were not yet wise enough to know that acting wise was not wise. They thought they were expected to know it all, and not knowing, they bluffed.

"The problem extends further than crows alone," Crow suggested.

"There are apparently some indications of that," the elder said, examining his underwings for parasites.

"Has the council met to debate the matter?" Crow asked.

"No!" the elder said sharply. "To panic the population with premature and unsubstantiated charges would be irresponsible. I see no reason to alarm the members of this rookery with dubious facts."

"The fact that birds of all kinds are dying wholesale is not dubious, elder," Crow exhorted.

"As the eldest elder," the young oldest elder said, his tone threatening, "I will tolerate no sensationalism here. There's been enough of that in the past, yearling. When you are as old as I and you've seen all I have seen, you'll understand. My responsibility is onerous. Being at the top is a lonely station. I am thrust into this position of leadership by circumstance, but my loyalty to this flock is paramount. After I—and a few other elders—have examined the problem thoroughly, then we will issue a directive. Until then, there will be no, I repeat, *no* rumor-spreading, which merely incites the more volatile elements of the community Is that clear?"

"Yes," Crow fumed.

"We have enough trouble with social unrest, disparate factions, and crowd control as it is," the elder expounded.

"Thank you, elder," Crow said. Thereupon he took wing and returned to his own roost.

But no statement or directive was forthcoming. The elders were busy reinstituting the sentry system which had been abandoned during winter. They held forth on many subjects and arbitrated countless pecking-order disputes. All the while, their members died in mounting numbers.

As Crow had said, it was not a problem confined to birds alone. He made exploratory flights, visiting swamps, marshes, and coastline areas. He found unexplained deaths among animals of all kinds. He approached the young oldest elder anew.

"Sparrows, robins, seagulls, and fish crows are dying too," Crow related.

"Good riddance to the sparrows," the elder snorted.

"The peril is widespread, elder," Crow insisted. "We should call a general meeting and debate the cause. We can't continue to ignore it! Every day more of our flock dies. These dead have no wounds, no bleeding, no external signs of illness, but dead they are."

"A virus, most likely," the elder said, shifting uneasily. "It'll run its course; such things always do. Those who survive will be stronger for it."

"What if none of us survive?" Crow questioned.

"We always have," the elder said testily. "We always will."

"Elder," Crow said, his tone too sharp, "to do nothing is a mistake!"

Whack! The elder's beak cracked Crow on the skull so hard it sent him spiraling off the limb.

"We'll have none of your impertinence, yearling," the elder commanded. "When we have something positive to say, we will say it. Hereafter I will thank you to keep your infantile observations to yourself."

Crow regained his perch, seething. Had it not been for the serious social disorder he might have created, Crow would have attacked the elder that instant. But the belief was bone-deep in him: right or wrong, just or not, a community with no chain of command fell into chaos. He could not bring himself to disrupt the system out of personal vengeance.

"I apologize, elder. I was disrespectful."

"Away with you," the elder ordered.

"Yes, elder."

Relating this to the four armadillos, Crow vented his anger verbally. Politely, Dill listened until Crow's diatribe ebbed and then, sympathetically, the armadillos invited Crow to share a bit of the ever-present carrion they were finding.

"You shouldn't eat carrion now, Dill!" Crow protested.

"Why not?" Dill asked, his thoughts syncopated by four mouths chewing at once.

"There may be something that carries over to you in such creatures," Crow persisted. "It might make you ill!"

"Maybe so," Dill said nonchalantly, "but those of us who take carrion regularly would be less likely to be harmed than those of you who take it infrequently, don't you think?"

"I don't know," Crow confessed, "but I wouldn't want to lose you, Dill. Not one of you."

Touched, the armadillos trundled toward their burrow. It wasn't hunger that made them eat in the first place.

"We were just stuffing," Dill said. "Eat less, live longer, that's what we'll do, Crow. We don't want to worry you."

"I *am* worried," Crow said, watching the foursome dig out soil so their soft undersides would be next to cool, fresh dirt.

"I think we should have a meeting among us thinkers," Crow declared suddenly. "This doesn't affect only crows. Many types of animals are dying."

"A meeting?" Dill chorused.

"Great grubs, Dill!" Crow exclaimed, now quite taken with his own idea. "We might alter the course of natural history—do you realize that? We could tackle any problem with our universal knowledge, and we could—"

"With our what?"

"Universal knowledge," Crow said absently, thinking of the ramifications of his idea.

"What, please tell, is a 'universal knowledge?' " Dill questioned, each quadruplet squinting at Crow.

"The source of all knowledge," Crow said, returning from his reverie.

"How does it work?" Dill asked.

Crow remembered that, with four brains combined, Dill was far smarter than any one armadillo, but still considerably less so than Lotor or himself.

"It's a mental exercise," Crow explained carefully. "It requires supreme concentration and is very hazardous to those who undertake it, leaving the body unprotected for extended periods of time."

"Oh, gnats!" Dill said. "Concentration?"

"I wouldn't worry about it," Crow said with sudden inspiration. "We'll need some responsible guard watching the bodies when we leave them."

The idea excited Dill to such a degree that even with all four minds coalescing, they stuttered, "Su-su-sure! You can't leave a b-b-body unattended, can you? All kinds of things could happen, right? Su-su-sure!"

"I'll round up Lotor," Crow said. "See if you can find Adam. We'll meet back here tomorrow. It'll take that long for Lotor to come from the far side of the marsh, if that's where he is."

"Sassafras!" Dill whooped, scurrying together. "We'll do it!"

With the largest adrenal glands of any animal, proportionate to their size, Dill was capable of extraordinary bursts of energy. An armadillo can, for example, disappear before your eyes in soft soil, all four legs digging furiously at once. Properly motivated, the armored creatures could move at truly astonishing speeds—although, with their restricted vision, it was not exactly wise for them to do so. But now, induced by the excitement of Crow's idea, Dill raced across the field. Crow had to laugh aloud. From the air, the quadruplets looked like four stones crisscrossing one another's paths, racing away with no notion as to where they were going.

As for himself, Crow had the advantage of flight. He was soon over Lotor's territory, seeking the raccoon's den.

Since Dill had not met Lotor, introductions were in order. With that amenity out of the way, Crow spoke of the widespread deaths as the rattlesnake, raccoon, and armadillos listened.

"What do you propose?" Lotor queried.

"A pool of our minds," Crow explained. "While we leave our bodies with Dill, let us all train our thoughts to the universal wave and try to find out what is happening."

It took several minutes to convince Lotor of the dependability of the foursome. With Adam vouching for them, based on his winter in their den, and with Crow's own personal high praise of the armadillos, Lotor yielded.

"I don't want to return and find myself without a viable body, you understand," Lotor said to Dill.

"Needless to say," Dill agreed, deeply moved by the testimonials of Crow and Adam, "we'll guard your body with our lives; you may be sure of that."

"Uh, little consolation is drawn from that, actually," Lotor said. "But little more could be expected, I suppose."

"May I suggest that you take advantage of Dill's burrow?" Crow offered. "Both you and Adam would be safe there, Lotor."

"Su-su-superb!" Dill squealed. "Good thinking!"

Lotor tuned his thoughts to a level beyond Dill's ability to comprehend. "Why aren't they joining this exercise, Crow?"

"They can't. Together as four, they barely make one, don't you see? Please, Lotor, be kind to them. They mean well, and they're terribly loyal and generous."

"I didn't catch that, Crow," Dill said cheerfully.

"Nothing, Dill," Crow said. "We were just trying to get our minds in gear for the project."

"Oh." A touch of disappointment.

Lotor proceeded to impress the armadillos with the importance of their job. He explained about the constant hum they could expect to hear. He told them how crucial it was never to leave the apparently lifeless bodies untended. Nor should they try to move the bodies except in a dire emergency. Building up the armadillos, bolstering their sense of responsibility, he imbued the quadruplets with the pride of purpose essential to safety.

Turning now to Crow, Lotor asked, "How do you suggest we approach this entrancement?"

"I really don't know," Crow admitted.

"May I offer a suggestion?" Adam advanced timidly.

"Certainly, Adam."

"Let us go our own way, each of us seeking whatever information we might gather. Since none of us have undertaken this sort of entrancement before, we have no idea where we're going or what to anticipate."

"That sounds reasonable to me," Lotor announced.

"And to me," Crow said.

The raccoon and rattlesnake were entering Dill's burrow when it occurred to everyone that no thought had been given to Crow's body placement!

"We can't climb trees, Crow!" Dill wailed, foreseeing a cancellation of the plan even before its initiation.

"Come into the burrow with us," Lotor recommended.

"No," Crow said, his craw tightening at the prospect of being underground. Dens had no appeal to crows.

"Then how can we protect you?" Dill cried.

"I'll be all right," Crow said, trying to cover the truly frightening thoughts he was harboring. He couldn't afford to foster any negative waves now!

"I'll take a position next to the trunk of this tree, higher up," Crow said, firmly. "I'll clamp my toes extra tight so I can't possibly fall. It's highly unlikely that I will be seen, since I'll be motionless. All Dill has to do is keep some predator from climbing the tree."

The horrible thought of facing a predator trying to attack the immobile body of their friend Crow made the weaponless armadillos seriously consider dropping the plan.

"Everything will be all right!" Crow said more forcefully. "Let's get on with it now."

Less positive than a moment ago, they each settled down in

their respective areas. The rattlesnake took the same den he'd had the previous winter. Lotor chose a more shallow berth. Crow put a clamp to his toes he'd never used before.

After a few false starts and nervous regroupings, they began.

PART TWO
Peregrinations

XI

Dill's entrance and exit from the burrow was performed in silence. Preoccupied with the responsibility bestowed on them, the armadillos monitored their charges constantly. Checking the deeper burrow taken by Adam, then the other, higher level where Lotor lay immobile, the armadillos worried. Lotor had told them to expect a hum. It was there. Reverberating against the clay walls of the tunnels, the drone gave Dill no comfort.

In and out the four of them went, posting one of their number at the mouth of the burrow as the other three foraged. All the while, they were acutely concerned with the crow, somewhere beyond their field of vision up a tree. Strain as they might to hear a hum from there, no sound reached their ears. The only thing they could do was defend zealously the base of the tree against trespass. Fortunately, no danger had yet appeared.

By the end of the third day and second night, the armadillos were becoming anxious. Nothing had changed. The animals below continued to drone and Crow's body was still on the roost overhead. But such a long time without food!

Despite their anxiety, the ordeal continued for the quadruplets. Other than the humming, no sign of life emanated from the rattlesnake and raccoon. Dill could only assume it was the same with their friend Crow.

From tissue to tendon to blood and the heart, through marrow and bone to the system of nerves, Crow traced not one body but many. Into kidneys, lungs, and livers, like a microbe he went, searching hundreds of victims for a clue.

He examined the four kinds of feathers: contour, down, filoplume, and powderdown. From filament to follicle to epidermal tissues he went inward to involuntary, myocardall, and voluntary musculature. He covered the smooth, striated, and cardiac functions of the body fibers.

Working in concentric circles, ever inward, the repetitious examinations began to bear fruit as Crow discovered first one, then two, and finally many similarities among cadavers. From the warm-blooded mammals to the cold of reptiles and fish, Crow traversed the span of the animal kingdom. He was here, there, everywhere at once. So focalized was his attention to the problem, he knew nothing else.

The marvels of a single cell enthralled him. Here in the basic structural unit of all life he observed the division and development of one cell from a preexisting one. Therein he found the chromosomes, with their prestamped genes, that determined all hereditary factors. And there he found a clue.

Following an intricate chain of food and source, his search took him to swamp and highland, creek and river. As he examined first one animal and then another, he was drawn to the lowest forms of life. Link after link of the food chain fell into place. Finally he reached the first, ominous stone upon which it had all begun. Like an inverted pyramid, the first "stone" supported all the other connecting ones.

His conscious mind hovered over an algae-green pond located behind a factory with huge smokestacks thrust high into the sky. The factory produced disinfectants and pesticides. Care had been taken to block the pouring of waste into the Tombigbee River, which became Mobile Bay several miles farther south. But from the back of the settling ponds a steady seepage had found its way into the streams that ran like capillaries away from the river and then ultimately back into the same river far downstream.

Crow gathered the straggling remnants of his thoughts, pulling himself from every distant point to which he had sent his mind. Into his body came the firm beat of an awakening heart. His temperature rose to normal. His mind climbed from the depths of slumber to dim awareness. Slowly, carefully, he reassembled himself.

Dill's joy at seeing the crow was boundless. The quadruplets tumbled, tittered, talked constantly, and had an overwhelming desire to sniff Crow, as though to be certain he was really there, safe, sound, and healthy. Crow permitted this. He departed briefly to stuff his craw, thankful that food was easy to find these days. On his return, neither Lotor nor Adam had yet awakened. Crow took up vigil with the armadillos.

"Are they still humming?" Crow asked at one point.

"Steadily."

"Good," Crow said. Despite the sleeplike state of entrancement, he was exhausted. He spent the next two days doing nothing but eating and sleeping, awakening now and then to find Dill talking. The armadillos were vociferous beyond their normal selves, induced in part by their desire to make sure Crow did not slip back into an unplanned entrancement so soon after returning.

"You all right, Crow?"

"Fine, Dill."

"You didn't answer," Dill said reprovingly.

"I must've dozed off. I'm sorry."

"It's okay," Dill said, all four bodies relaxing now. "It wasn't really important," they added softly.

The initial signs of awakening came first in Lotor. One of the armadillos came barreling out of the burrow, agog with excitement.

"He's moving!"

"Who's moving?" Crow asked.

"The raccoon! He's stretching his toes and his fur is beginning to bristle as though he were moving it."

"Good," Crow said. "It won't be long now."

"Check the snake—" All four armadillos ran back underground.

When they reappeared, they confirmed it. "Lotor's waking up, but Adam's still not moving."

"Is there a hum?" Crow asked.

"Yes, Adam's humming."

"Then don't worry," Crow said. "All we need do now is wait."

The awakening process took most of the morning. By early afternoon Lotor's breathing was deep and regular, Dill reported. The hum was gone. The raccoon slept the more natural sleep of a creature spent.

"He doesn't usually move around too much by day anyway," Crow remarked, calming Dill's exuberant questions regarding the raccoon.

"Maybe we should wake him just a teeny bit to see if he's all right," Dill suggested.

"I don't think so, Dill. Let him sleep. He'll wake in due time."

"Maybe nudge him to see if he grunts?" Dill asked.

"I don't believe so, Dill. Let's just wait."

So they waited. Another entire day, they waited. It was late afternoon of the following day before Lotor ambled out of the burrow, his hair on one side matted and crumpled oddly by the prolonged dormancy. Squinting his masked eyes, Lotor acknowledged the presence of the four armadillos and Crow. "You did good," Lotor rumbled. With that, he waddled off in search of sustenance.

A day later, Adam came out of the burrow and, without a single thought in passing, went looking for food.

"What's going on?" Dill complained.

"They'll be back," Crow said.

"No word, no nothing!" Dill cried. "Is there going to be a meeting? Anything?"

"It won't be long," Crow said calmly.

"Adam didn't say a thing!"

"He's very slow to warm up, Dill."

"Not even a passing hiss!"

"He doesn't mean to be rude, I'm sure," Crow said.

"Well, really!" Dill said, distressed at the sagging climax to the entrancement. "Is that all there is to it?"

"No," Crow placated, "there'll be a report when Adam and Lotor return."

"Gnats!" Dill fumed. "Not even a hiss!"

Crow took wing, himself going for food, his mind still afar, thinking of all he had seen and learned. He spent a solitary afternoon, perfunctorily pecking up seed corn that had dribbled from a planter. At the far end of the same field the mechanical instrument chugged along, poking seeds into freshly turned soil, the human watching his furrows and oblivious to a single black figure nibbling up stray kernels.

Night found Crow sitting on the limb above Dill's burrow, awaiting the return of Adam and Lotor. Adam was the first to make an appearance, his elongated body bulging with the repast just consumed. He came after dark and secreted himself beneath a low shrub nearby. Lotor arrived the following evening.

"We are all assembled," Crow noted.

The four armadillos waited with obvious impatience. Adam crawled out into the open and Crow alighted near a mound of scooped earth from the burrow.

"I found the cause of the deaths," Crow announced.

"Good!" Dill exclaimed.

There was no outburst from Adam and Lotor. They listened as Crow outlined the sequence of events that ultimately ended in the widespread demise of so many creatures.

"It's called 'mercury,' " Crow related, his thought a monotone. "It accumulates in shellfish, which in turn are consumed by other sea life, which in their turn fall prey to sea birds, larger fish, carrion-eaters, and so forth. Down the chain of food and supply comes the mercury, passing from one ingested system to the next and constantly accumulating in the kidneys of any animal who has eaten it. It produces loose teeth, fever, urinary difficulties, nausea, diarrhea, sore tongue, impaired eyesight, and brain damage in some animals —and finally paralysis, increasing weakness, and death. The heavier the body weight of the victim, the longer it takes to be fatal. Body chemistry is a factor.

"The effect is assiduous," Crow said, "building in the system of everything in this area that swims in water so affected, or anything that eats something so poisoned."

"What can we do about it?" Dill asked, when Crow had finished.

"I'm not sure," Crow said. "Stop eating certain foods, possibly."

"There's more to it," Lotor said.

Slowly, with the same humdrum manner of reporting that Crow had exhibited, the raccoon began his report. "The poison comes in many forms, Crow. It is sprinkled in the human fields to kill insects, retard weed growth, and eliminate pests. When it rains, the residue is carried to every stream. Any grain planted may have been sprayed with a like poison to keep borers or fungus from attacking it."

Adam the rattlesnake sighed. "It's in the air we breathe as well."

The third report was equally as pessimistic. Adam said, "It's a powder that on a given day is inhaled by everything that breathes. Particles of matter are in every breath of air. This is just as dangerous as the poisoned fields and sea life because it, too, accumulates with time, minute portions of the dust emptying poison directly into the blood system. Thereby it enters every part of the body and attacks the cells themselves."

"This is very depressing," Dill said, promptly becoming depressed.

"It's in the food we eat, the air we breathe, the land we stand on," Lotor concluded. "It's in the flesh of our prey and the foliage on which they graze. There's no way to escape it."

"What can we do?" Dill wailed.

There was no reply. The armadillos looked from Crow to Adam to Lotor and nothing was said.

111

"We can't do anything?" Dill questioned in a small voice. "Are we doomed?"

"I'm afraid there's more," Lotor said.

"More?" Crow asked.

"It's not only here, around us. There are similar things happening for a great distance—as far as I went in my entrancement. I found freshwater fish dying in Colorado, large pronghorn deer almost wiped out in the Rockies, crocodiles endangered in the Everglades, many species very near complete eradication. They are not all dying for the same reasons."

"This is so," Adam affirmed. "I found the same."

"How—how far does this go?" Crow questioned.

"Jungles, mountains, plains, deserts, forests," Lotor replied.

"Deep in caves, underwater, at the North and South poles," Adam continued.

"In the deepest oceans and seas," Lotor intoned, his words the mood of a requiescat.

"From here to land's end, from continent to continent," Lotor whispered.

"Burrowers, swimmers, fliers, climbers, walkers, crawlers—" Adam rejoined.

"Nothing," Lotor choked, "nothing is exempt."

Stunned, the animals sat unmoving for a very long time. Each with private thoughts, although all the others might hear them, considered the staggering news they had learned. Dill, of course, was twice baffled. Deserts? Oceans? Crocodiles? Dill had no inkling what existed outside his observation.

"Everything?" Dill asked, breaking the silence.

"Everything," Lotor and Adam replied in unison.

"All over, everywhere?" Dill pressed. "Is there no safe place we could go?"

"It is the prophecy," Crow said softly.

"What can we do?" Dill questioned, his tone panicky. "We have to eat; we have to have water! We have to breathe, don't we? What can any of us do?"

Lotor arose and began to walk away.

"Wait a minute, Lotor!" Dill called. "Let's figure out something we can do. Lotor? Come on back and let's see what you fellows can figure out here. Lotor!"

The raccoon gave no reply, disappearing in the dark.

"Maybe we can figure out something by ourselves," Dill said, addressing Crow and Adam. "Whattayasay, thinkers? Let's put our heads together and see what we can decide."

Adam slowly uncoiled and, with undulating movements of his ribs, stole away, Dill calling after him, "Come on, Adam, whattayasay? Whattayasay, Adam?"

Adam said nothing.

Disconsolately Dill looked up at the crow, black feathers in a dark night and now settling onto a roost for sleep.

"Crow?"

"Yes, Dill?"

"Can thinkers solve problems like this, Crow?"

"We'll try, Dill," Crow said, closing his eyes and sighing.

"Sure we can!" Dill said in harmony. "Us thinkers can whip this problem—right, Crow?"

Crow's breathing was slow and shallow. He was asleep.

"Can't we, Crow?" Dill asked.

No reply.

The armadillos wandered off, one behind the other, looking for edibles. Through the night their thoughts took a pattern they'd never collectively experienced. Each of the four asked questions of the other, their minds working as individuals.

"Wu-wu-we can do it!"

113

"Su-su-sure we can!"

"We can!"

One lone thought, and none of them was sure which of their brains sent it: "C-c-can't we?"

"Sure we can!" Together.

"C-c-can't we?"

XII

For several days, Crow waited. Neither Adam nor Lotor returned to the armadillo burrow, so Crow went looking for the raccoon.

Lotor preferred free-running streams and the foods to be found in them; his den would be nearby. Crow discovered mussel shells, five-toed prints, and shredded logs, but no Lotor. Although the raccoon seldom ate more than a pound of food in a day, he was an insatiable nibbler. His hunger satisfied, Lotor meddled—drawing tactile pleasure from fondling shiny stones, peeking under rocks, and hole-poking. Any choice morsel was thoroughly chewed, Lotor's forty teeth grinding it to the point of evaporation, savoring the taste even when the bulk was not needed. Only chimpanzees, porpoises, man, and some birds could surpass Lotor's vocal abilities. The raccoon's chirping, churring, purring, staccato expressions were audible indications of mood. Seldom hurried, enjoying everything around him, Lotor was every inch the philosopher.

From one hollowed tree to another, Crow sought telltale grey and black hairs around any likely hole. He intruded on several families in a common den and was promptly evicted from their sanctuary.

Raccoons are not mature until age two; therefore it wasn't likely that the season was influencing Lotor's activity. For this reason, Crow avoided dens where markings indicated several raccoons were in residence. Boars were usually loners except in breeding season. It was safe to assume Lotor was content with solitude.

It was in the hour of half-light at dawn when Crow found the burly raccoon, shuffling plantigrade fashion, head down, sniffing.

"Hello, Lotor!" Crow hailed.

As though they had not been apart, Lotor asked, "Do you hear that cricket, Crow?"

"Yes I do, Lotor."

"I've been hunting that cricket for days," Lotor said, combing the grass. "I come by here on my way to bed and he fiddles like mad. Do you think he's taunting me?"

"I doubt it, Lotor," Crow surmised. "Insects are slaves to instinct, and they don't think at all."

"If I find him, I'll get a tasty treat. You ever eat crickets?"

"Sometimes," Crow said. "When I can catch them."

"They make that *riberty-riberty* sound with their hind legs, did you know that?" Lotor mused. He hovered over a piece of limb, ready to pounce when he turned it over. Nothing but a worm. He ate it.

"Listen, Lotor," Crow said, "why didn't you come back to the armadillo den so we could go on with the entrancement?"

"I'm through with all that, Crow," Lotor said.

"Through with entrancement?" Crow asked incredulously.

"Wait a minute! I think I've spotted the little morsel. Listen!"

Crow held his thoughts as Lotor balanced on his rear legs and studied the area, head atilt, front feet poised and out-stretched. "Guess not," Lotor concluded. He continued his search.

"You don't really mean you're not going to entrance your-self anymore, do you?" Crow questioned.

"Yep. Giving it up."

"But why?"

"What's the future in it, Crow?" Lotor asked. He halted a moment, glancing at Crow, then turned back to hunting.

"Future? I don't understand."

"Will it fill our bellies?" Lotor asked, hands busy parting grass. "Will it kill mites and ticks? Will it stop what's happen-ing? Can we do anything about it? I mean anything at *all*?"

"You said yourself, Lotor—it's the way to all knowledge."

"Yes, well, there are some things I'd just as soon not know, Crow."

"Like what?" Crow asked, his tone taking an edge of disap-proval.

"Like about crawdads, Crow," Lotor said, his own tone sharper. "I got to thinking about crawdads. It depressed me. It got to where crawdads didn't taste so good—and I'll tell you, Crow, when you mess yourself up so you don't enjoy craw-dads, you're messed up!"

"But you know they're full of mercury," Crow protested.

"Wait a minute!" Lotor snapped. "I don't want to hear about it, Crow. You understand? I don't want to think about it. I can't taste the mercury, if it is there. The crawdad tastes mighty juicy to me, and I'm not going to ruin my enjoyment by sitting around letting juicy crawdads go by."

117

"I can't believe this," Crow whispered. "You're a thinker, Lotor. You know what will happen to your liver and your—"

"Shut up!" Lotor snarled, whirling to face Crow.

"Lotor!" Crow's tone rose. "If you were some dumb beast without a thought in your head, that'd be one thing. But you have intelligence and insight. Are you telling me you will go on eating poison? Knowing it's poison, you'll eat it? The crawdads are full of—"

Lotor sprang at Crow, hissing, black lips curled. "Shut up, Crow! Keep your thoughts to yourself!"

The two stared at one another. Lotor's fury abated and Crow began anew, his tone more even. "Very well, Lotor. If crawdads mean that much to you."

Lotor abandoned the still-chirping cricket and ambled down a poorly defined path. Crow knew the raccoon was headed for den and bed.

"I need your help, Lotor," Crow said, following.

"To do what?"

"To look for a way to overcome what's happening."

"No future in it, Crow."

"We might be able to figure something, between you, Adam, and me," Crow insisted.

"Against humans?" Lotor snorted.

"We don't know until we try, do we?" Crow said.

"Don't be a fool," Lotor grunted, ascending the trunk of his tree.

"Well, Lotor, we might!"

Lotor squeezed through the hole of his den, somersaulting so that he came up with his nose poking out again. Crow lit on a nearby limb.

"Listen, Crow," Lotor said, his tone strangely alien, "let me tell you how it is. I didn't go into detail when we came back from entrancement, because there's no point going into it. We can't make the sun stop shining. We can't make clouds hold the rain. We can't stave off winter. And we can't do a thing about what's happening. There's nothing I can do."

"But you don't know until we try!"

"Don't keep saying that!" Lotor barked. "There's nothing any of us can do! Dill was right: we have to eat, drink, and breathe. Period. If giving up crawdads would save us, I'd do it. But if crawdads don't get you, mutated insects will. If insects don't get you, the water will. If the water doesn't get you . . ." Lotor's voice trailed off. Then, with a sigh: "I don't want to think about it."

"Don't you see, this is why we need to undergo entrancement again and again, Lotor," Crow implored.

"Not me."

"What's going to save us, then?"

"Not me," Lotor grumped. "Nor you, for that matter."

"Lotor, I can't believe that a creature as wise as you, as smart as—"

"Go away, Crow," Lotor said wearily. "There's nothing I can do."

For a long time, the two looked at one another. Then, hesitantly, Crow pursued the subject. "If you won't undergo entrancement again, can you tell me what you saw? There must be a way to circumvent these things."

When Lotor did not respond, Crow asked again, "Could you tell me what you saw, Lotor?"

"What I saw?" Lotor intoned. "Sure, Crow, I could tell you what I saw."

Silence.

Then Crow asked, "Will you tell me, Lotor?"

"I don't want to, Crow."

"Lotor," Crow's tone trembled, "If you do nothing, if I do nothing, if we refuse even to think about it, we are as guilty as

119

if we observed a predator and gave no warning! The least you could do is tell me."

"Go see for yourself," Lotor said.

"I might not see what you saw!"

That was truth and Lotor knew it. His black eyes stared across the marshy terrain, his brain flickering unpleasant sensations.

"Lotor?"

"What I saw, Crow," Lotor said, very very softly, "was doom."

Gently, Crow urged, "Tell me, Lotor."

Lotor's eyes were distant, mirroring the shimmering orb of a rising sun now pulling free of the horizon.

"Have you ever seen a short-tailed albatross, Crow?" Without response, Lotor continued, "It has a wingspread of seven feet. Dark wings and white body. He spends his entire life at sea, returning to land only during the breeding season. They once ranged the world. Eskimos and Indians killed and ate them along the coast of California, Oregon, and Alaska only a few years ago. They don't anymore, though. At one time the short-tailed albatross nested on the Pacific islands of Kobishi, Nishi-no-shima, and Kita-no-shima. Then along came human progress."

Crow waited. So long he waited that he had to urge, "Go on, Lotor."

"The short-tailed albatross was driven from its nesting grounds by humans who came—not because they were hungry—but for feathers. Then there was only one island left where the short-tailed albatross went; it barely survived, but somehow it did. The island was rocked by volcanic eruptions, the nesting grounds were destroyed again and again, but the short-tailed albatross somehow held on. Again came man. Humans reduced their numbers from half a million

120

birds to ten breeding pairs, Crow. Only then man began to protect them."

"Well, good!" Crow exclaimed.

Lotor's tone was unchanged. "The female short-tailed albatross produces one egg a year. It takes a year for the young to fly, and the fledgling will have been out of the nest nine years before it returns to breed."

Crow stared at Lotor.

"Say good-bye to the short-tailed albatross, Crow," Lotor said. "They don't stand a chance."

"Lotor, Lotor," Crow said gently, "the extinction of a single bird is sad, but it isn't the end of the world!"

"Say good-bye, Crow." Lotor's voice was a monotone. "Good-bye to the wolves of Europe—they're already gone. Wolves in America can't last much longer. Already the plains wolves have all been killed. The eastern timber wolf is about to go. Only a few left, mostly in Alaska, and humans still pay a bounty to hunters for every pelt. Say good-bye to the heath hen, Crow; it's extinct. Stellar's seacow, Caribbean monk seal, eastern cougar, Merriman elk—going or gone, all of them. California condor, black-footed ferret, key deer, Columbian white-tailed deer, Sonoran pronghorn, Florida crocodile, and the manatee . . . three-spined stickleback, Colorado River squawfish, Piute cutthroat, pike, and Devil's Hole pupfish . . . the striped bass and shad . . . prairie chicken . . . auk . . . Carolina parakeets. Gone, or soon to be."

Stunned, Crow sat motionless as Lotor's now expressionless tone revealed what entrancement had shown. "For nine million years the sandhill crane flew over this continent," Lotor related, "surviving disease, predators, and natural disasters—for *nine million years!* They lay only two eggs a year, and they can't do that without marshlands. Humans not only take high land, they fill in the low.

"Whales once found in herds of a hundred now exist in seas where they can't find mates," Lotor said. "Galapagos turtles . . . and tigers, Crow! Seven species of tiger all about gone. Not just here or there, but over the whole world— Balinese, Javan, Caspian, Siberian, Chinese, Bengal, and Sumatran tigers, Crow."

"But why?" Crow cried.

"Fur," Lotor said mechanically. "One coat for a human takes six leopards, Crow. Already the Asiatic cheetah is gone. Soon the jaguar and ocelot."

"Not everything has fur, Lotor!" Crow said. "Not everything is dying for its fur!"

"No," Lotor agreed, his voice distant. "Some die for food, some for their feathers, some because the creature is feared. Others because they're considered pests. They die for many reasons. Or no reason, like the mercury poisoning."

"Lotor?"

A long pause. "Yes?"

"Is there nothing that can be done?"

Long pause. "Nothing."

"There must be something, Lotor."

"No."

"If we entrance ourselves, it's better than doing nothing, isn't it?"

"No."

"Why?" Crow shrilled.

Lotor covered his eyes with both forefeet and massaged his face a few moments. He yawned. "I must go to sleep, Crow. I've been up all night."

"Lotor! We must do something!"

Lotor's tone was less patient. "My life may be thirteen years long, at best. The *average* raccoon lives seven to ten years, Crow. Those are the lucky ones. My brother was grabbed by a bobcat. We all face a dubious future. The ratio of newborns to mating age varies, but survival is not the rule, Crow, it's the exception. There is nothing we can do about what I saw. *Nothing*. Do you hear me, Crow? Nothing! As for me, I am not going to deprive myself of crawdads. Ridiculous! Life is too short."

"Think of every generation that follows us, Lotor!"

"They'll shift for themselves, Crow," Lotor said, tersely. "Our ancestors did nothing for us. Our heirs will blame us no more."

"Lotor?"

Sharply, "What is it, Crow?"

"What'll happen, finally?"

"How finally?"

"Finally," Crow said. "At last."

Lotor sighed heavily and looked at Crow. "You must enjoy the suffering of knowledge. Why do you worry about a time after you're dead and gone?"

"I—I'm not sure why, Lotor. But I do. Maybe because the extinction of a species is the final demise of every ancestor which created it. Somehow my death alone is not so final. But for all crows to be gone!"

"You don't want to know, Crow."

"Tell me."

"Go away, I need to sleep."

"Lotor, please!"

"They'll kill us all, Crow," Lotor snapped. "For food, profit, or sport. Because we're pests or because they fear us. Or because they don't know what they're doing. But they'll kill us all!"

"I—I can't believe that, Lotor."

"They'll dam rivers, heat streams, they'll do it by accident, maybe, like the mercury. Now go away—I want to sleep."

123

"You refuse to help seek a solution, Lotor?" Crow asked.

"There's nothing—" Lotor's head came out the hole of his den and he spoke slowly, emphatically. "There is nothing you can do, Crow. Nothing. Nothing. Are you deaf? There's nothing we can do!"

"Lotor, humans can't live without us."

"That's true." Lotor burrowed into his nest.

"They'll have killed themselves, too."

"True, Crow." Irritated. "Will you get away from me?"

"I can't sit by and do nothing, Lotor."

"Suit yourself. Go away."

"There has to be a way to stop what's happening."

"Go eat a crawdad, Crow. You'll feel better."

On leaden wings, Crow departed. How could Lotor refuse to participate? How could any creature refuse to save his own kind? Flying with no purpose, or so it seemed, Crow saw nothing, heard nothing, thinking. Something deep inside his brain, in the back of his mind, turned his flight toward Adam.

There had to be a way.

They could do it.

"Su-su-sure they could!"

XIII

After several minutes of hypertense rattling which erupted with Crow's sudden appearance, Adam composed himself and settled down. He stared at Crow with the unnerving gaze found only in serpents. On either side of his face were heat-sensitive pits which gave him the appearance of having four nostrils.

"I've been talking to Lotor," Crow said. "We discussed his entrancement and what he learned."

Adam's tongue waved slowly, his keel-scaled body blending into the dappled shadows of a palmetto frond.

"Lotor says we're all doomed," Crow said. "I'd like your opinion."

"Lotor's right," Adam responded, the thought timorous despite his apparent composure.

"I can't bring myself to accept that," Crow said. "I think we should make an attempt to alter the course of things to come."

"How?" Adam asked.

"I don't know yet," Crow confessed. "But surely we can find a way."

"I doubt it," Adam said.

"It would be foolish to sit and accept defeat, would it not?" Crow questioned.

The reptile's body rose and fell with long, slow inhalations. Crow caught thoughts which were not aimed at communication as Adam debated with himself. "There's nothing we can do, Crow."

"Come on, Adam," Crow urged. "What can we lose by trying?"

"We would become acutely unhappy by obsessing ourselves with the inevitable," Adam deduced. "To face odds, no matter how great, where there's a faint glimmer of hope is one thing. In this case, there is no hope. Didn't Lotor tell you that?"

"He told me."

"He's right," Adam said.

Crow shifted from one foot to the other. Standing on flat ground is not a favored position with perching birds. But he wanted to be near enough to establish rapport with Adam.

"Lotor says he's giving up entrancement," Crow said.

"I see." Noncommittal.

"How do you feel about that, Adam? Will you give up entrancement?"

"No." Adam's tone was distant.

"Good!" Crow said. "Think we could undergo another entrancement and seek solutions—"

"A serpent is somewhat localized," Adam said. "I rarely venture farther than necessary to secure food and water. Immediately after eating, if it's a good-size meal, I'll lie as long as fifteen days while the food digests. It's—lonely."

Looking for the point of this, Crow said, "I can see that it would be."

"In the colder months," Adam continued, "I get sluggish as my body cools."

"Yes?"

"Winter makes me immobile."

"I know, Adam."

"Snakes aren't gregarious, at least rattlers aren't," Adam noted. "About the only time we get together is for mating or to share a den, but it isn't a social thing; you understand?"

"I think so."

"For reptiles, it's a system that's worked for millions of years. Snakes are creatures of reaction, Crow. They don't think. When they're hungry they hunt, when they're thirsty they seek water, when sated they settle down until something else moves them to fill their needs."

Crow held his mind to neutral thoughts.

"When I discovered I was the only snake that had complete thoughts, it scared me," Adam said, his breathing now more rapid. "The prospect of living without speaking, without hearing, trapped in my own brain—my mind races around in here, Crow. I sit for days contemplating my life, and it is so *restricted*. I would feel the tremor of passing creatures and envy their mobility. Birds fly up so they can see the world. I'd give anything to be able to fly like you do."

Crow was stone-still, listening.

"When I met Lotor, I heard him thinking. My tail began—like it does—I thought this stupid rattle of mine was going to scare him away before I could communicate with him. Then Lotor realized what was happening in my head. Lotor is very wise."

"Yes."

"He enjoys talking," Adam said.

"He does that," Crow agreed.

"But I listen well," Adam continued, almost defensively. "Lotor likes a listener!"

"Adam—"

"We became friends almost at once," Adam explained.

Crow felt a change in the rattlesnake's emotions.

"I dreaded seeing him go away," Adam said. "I had terrible visions of Lotor getting hurt, or killed or just bored with me! Then the most wonderful thing happened."

Adam laughed and the sound was pleasing to Crow's mind.

"Lotor taught me about entrancement." Adam's thoughts lifted. "I could fly, Crow! I could see the world! Under oceans and over trees and into other creatures. Nothing was afraid of me and I feared nothing! I communed with minds continents away. I could hear birds calling, the howl of a canine, the purr of a cat. I hiss and I've felt myself hissing, but I'd never *heard* a hiss before! The world was a beautiful, vibrant place, Crow. Can you understand what I'm saying?"

"Adam, Adam—"

"Free," Adam whispered. "Untethered, unrestricted, un-afraid, un—unbelievable."

Adam's sides were heaving, the only external indication of what was happening in the serpent's mind.

"So I *can't* give up entrancement," Adam concluded. "I would sink my fangs in my own body first."

"Good, Adam," Crow said softly.

"But Crow," Adam said, the quaver returning to the reptile's tone, "I can't do again what we did together."

"You must, Adam!"

"No. I can't. It was too upsetting, Crow. There's no way to change what has been or will be."

"There must be a way," Crow insisted. "We can't know until we entrance ourselves again and search further."

Adam replied firmly, "Lotor is right. It's hopeless, Crow. You can see for yourself. Entrance yourself, you'll see how hopeless it is."

"Many creatures will become extinct!"

"Yes," Adam said.

"You still won't help?"

"My life is so confined, don't you see? To leave this fixed position, to go out and seek misery—I just can't do that. There are too many beautiful things to think about, Crow. Did you know there are places in the world where it never gets cold? Summer the whole year round!"

"Adam, please."

"Crow," Adam said sharply, "there is nothing we can *do!* Why do you insist on torturing yourself about the inevitable?"

"You're wrong, Adam."

"What makes you so sure you're right?" Adam retorted, his head lifting angrily.

"We are not mindless," Crow said. "Only mindless creatures blindly allow death to stalk them."

Adam's head drew back, muscles taut as he held the menacing pose. Then his body relaxed and his head lowered.

"It is a curse to see the future, Crow. But there is no point in doubling the curse by dwelling on it futilely. Have you paused to consider that perhaps it is not your place to meddle in a natural sequence of events?"

"There's nothing natural about a species becoming extinct," Crow stated.

"By what right do you assume to set the balance of nature, Crow?"

"Should I stand by and see nature unbalanced, Adam?"

"There is no imbalance in nature, Crow," Adam said.

"If snakes disappear, rodents will be rampant!" Crow argued.

"If rodents disappear, insects become master," Adam said. "In their absence the balance is altered, but never is it *unba-lanced*, Crow. Nature cannot be unbalanced. There is no such thing. Survival is the *exception*. Nothing—nothing—stays constant. One creature multiplies only as another is subtracted to yield territory. One animal divides and becomes two types pursuing separate food chains so each type can survive and expand. As one species rises, a competitor is edged out of existence. It is natural, Crow."

"You are wrong," Crow whispered.

"We shall see."

"Wrong, Adam."

"You fear the change of the masses when in fact they will change anyway," Adam said gently. "Perhaps it is the cause of the change you fear most. The sum is the same, in the end. The difference is only the distribution of survivors. Life is abbreviated at best, Crow. Enjoy it. Don't suffer needlessly."

"You refuse to help me?" Crow asked.

Adam sighed, a long-drawn, audible escape of air from his elongated esophagus.

"Crow, I cannot help you."

Crow winged his way toward the rookery, fuming, his mood bordering on despair. He considered going to the armadillos, but what could they do? If Crow truthfully displayed his feelings, it would merely upset the amiable brothers.

Frustration pulsed through Crow's body with every beat of his heart. He screamed aloud, "Cawt! Cawt! Cawt!"—a cry of anger and futility. Lotor, with his appetite for crawdads, and Adam, with a carefully structured rationalization, both excused themselves from responsibility!

If he must, Crow would do it alone, he vowed. Accost the elders, demand action!

Be calm. Be sensible. The penalty for belittling an elder was swift and certain. Even the youngest elder would not tolerate a yearling who challenged the older bird's position. What would a yearling know that the longer-lived bird did not know four-fold? The yearling's survival was attributed more to luck than wisdom.

To attack an elder, to physically assault him, would end in one of two ways: defeat for the elder and the chaotic upheaval of order therefrom or, more likely, the exile of the offending yearling. Neither end would serve Crow's purpose.

Nonetheless, it was Crow's duty to warn them.

Excited caws and happy cries came to Crow's ears as he approached the rookery. He circled down among much cheering, joining the perimeter crowd.

"What's happening?" Crow queried.

"The yearlings are announcing their names," an elder chuckled. "How about you, have you decided on yours?"

XIV

The announcement of names spanned several days. The ceremony was traditional. Each fledgling to have survived a twelfth month would ascend to a lofty perch and broadcast his chosen title. Immediately the rookery would burst into boisterous commentary on the appellation. Some names were quickly accepted. Some elicited jocular ribbing. Others, usually pompous ones, were hooted derisively and promptly replaced by the flock with a less pretentious designation. These hapless yearlings were destined to be known thereafter by such monikers.

"I am Meteor!" one egoist pronounced.

"Meteor?" the flock guffawed. "Meteor! Crow *Meteor*?"

"More like Crow Bellow, you mean," someone cackled.

"Yeah, that's it! Crow Bellow! Suits his loud mouth much better. Har har har! Crow Bellow it is."

The chagrined yearling dropped to a lower roost and perched there, sulking. The name was now his and he could only hope to bring the title respect someday.

One of the rare two-year-olds who had not named himself last year reached the apex of a towering slash pine.

"I am Crow Magnus!" he cried.

"Crow Magnus . . . Crow Magnus . . ." Yes, it had a good strong feel, and the two-year-old was an intelligent bird from a good family. The flock murmured approval.

Thus it went until every yearling had been named except those having second thoughts about their choice, or weaker members too timid to step forward. As the number of untitled fledglings dwindled, attention to them intensified. The flock began making recommendations, and it was an unusual crow that could escape having a name thrust on him.

"How about you?" an elder prompted Crow. "I'm surprised you haven't stepped forward before now."

Crow skirted the issue by asking some pointed questions about the continuing high mortality rate among the flock.

"Don't start that again," the elder commanded. "This is a time for gaiety and nest building. The community doesn't want doomsday speeches. They won't tolerate it, and neither will I."

With that, the elder transported himself to more cheerful company.

"Crow Melano!" a female yearling proclaimed. The flock mouthed the sound and a wave of approbation swept the rookery.

Crow spent each day listening to dozens of suggestions, fending off wisecrack nicknames that might stick if he weren't careful.

"Come, come, come, yearling!" an elder scolded. "We can't wait forever for a decision, you know. My experience with yearlings who take so long is not good. Inevitably they make bad selections."

"I'll think of something," Crow said.

"Better hurry it along, young crow," the elder warned. "Otherwise you may get a name that does not flatter your opinion of yourself. Such as Crow Cuss. Hey! That's catchy," the elder mused. "You just might get tagged with something like that. I think it's rather clever, myself."

It was the "clever" suggestions that Crow needed to avert. He knew what name he would take. The question was, how to keep it from being ridiculed and replaced with some offensive nickname. He temporized as long as possible. The conclusion came one evening as the flock returned to the rookery after a day of foraging.

"What say you, young crow?" someone yelled at Crow.

"How about it, yearling?"

"Got a good name yet? Ought to have, after thinking about it all this time."

Tittering rippled through the rookery, and Crow knew he would have to take a stand.

"Say, hey, fellow flockers, let's see what we can come up with for our indecisive yearling."

Crow didn't have much choice; he had to do something before they did it for him. He rose to the pinnacle of a tree and immediately he had the flock's attention.

"I wish to announce my name," Crow began, lifting his voice so all could hear.

"Don't be bashful, bird! Go right ahead!"

Crow waited for the laughter to subside.

If a name was accepted by the flock, there was only one reason the elders could reject it: if the name already belonged to another crow.

"Let's hear it, yearling!" a voice from a distant tree.

"I select this name," Crow said loudly, "because it was given to me in a dream."

134

That was not the truth, of course. But who would believe the truth?

"I am Crow Mayor!" Crow shouted.

Silence.

Absolute silence.

A breeze made the trees shrug foliage briefly, then settled again to—silence.

First as a murmur, growing like a distant storm, the flock stirred, muttered, shifted in place, whispered among themselves, grumbled and bristled, their initial reaction giving way to indignation.

"How dare you?" an elder cried.

"Blasphemy!" another shrilled.

"No respect for elders living or dead."

"Let me explain!" Crow yelled.

But they were not open for explanations. The flock was a roar of condemnation. "Sacrilege! Blasphemy!"

"I am Crow Mayor!" Crow repeated, his voice swept aside by a torrent of angry caws.

He could have yielded. By dropping down from the lofty rostrum, he would have signified surrender and the clamor would have dissipated. More than likely he would then be heckled, humiliated, and subjected to a series of derogatory nicknames until one stuck.

It was not so much fear of dishonor that kept him at the tip of the tree as smoldering anger and plain stubbornness.

"Fee! Fee! Fee!" Their cries rang in his ears. The flock moved in short, quick flights, drawing more tightly around Crow.

Cutting, cruel laughter bubbled out of the roiling sounds of the flock.

"Yeah, yeah, yeah, the son of a sparrow-lover!"

135

Like soot gathering in eddies of wind, they speckled the trees around Crow, the density of their numbers greatest in the oak upon which he still held his ground.

"Thinks he's an elder already . . . been trying to solve the woes of the rookery . . . loudmouth upstart . . . never did like that impious young—"

Crow held his head high, eyes flashing angrily, commanding the eminence upon which he perched.

"Loner . . . thinks he doesn't need anyone else . . . crazy!"

Crow clamped his toes as tightly as possible, then slowly began to spread his wings. Like a giant imago unfolding from its cocoon, Crow's wings extended, farther and farther, until every quill was separated from the next—and still his wings continued to lengthen. Crow held them as far out as his muscles would allow. Rigid as stone, he held the pose. The screams became a roar, then a rumble, and as he perched unmoved, wings fixed, the din began to diminish.

"Cawt! Cawt! Cawt!" Crow's voice caromed from land to sky and echoed away to infinity.

"Cawt! Cawt! Cawt!" he shrieked again.

The rookery shifted *en totum,* the rustle of their collective feathers louder now than their voices.

"You are dying of poison in foods which come from water," Crow intoned. "Carrion of animals which die from such food also carry the poison. The poison is called 'mercury' and it comes from streams and rivers. I am who I say I am: Crow Mayor."

An elder hop-stepped higher until he was almost even with Crow. "Tell me, yearling," the elder said, "how did you learn this—this poison stuff?"

"In a dream."

"In a dream?" the elder sneered. "Same way you were given your name. Nobody can refute a dream, can they?"

Laughter. The elder continued, "Mayor was my friend. Are you my friend?"

"You and Mayor were never friends," Crow said firmly.

"That," the elder said, "is proof enough for me! Mayor and I were as close as a double-yolk egg, yearling."

"You fought constantly over policies of running this rookery," Crow corrected. "You advocated strict penalties for transgressions and Mayor was more lenient."

Where would this fledgling have gotten such information? The elder knew it to be true. Mayor had not held these arguments in public—he was the type to draw a foe aside for private confrontations. No one else could possibly know—

"Mayor and I conferred often," the elder snorted.

"You argued often, elder," Crow said.

"You are a liar, upstart!"

Wings outspread, his head unmoving, Crow spoke in a matter-of-fact tone that had the ring of truth. "Mayor broke with you when you tried to split the community to establish a second rookery in fish crow country."

"A lie, yearling!"

"Would you like me to continue?" Crow asked quietly.

"I say cast this blasphemer out!" the elder screamed.

"Wait a minute," another elder said, coming up to join them. "Why are we getting so excited? So he says he's Crow Mayor. What do we care? It's about time we took an objective look at our deceased elder, Mayor."

The flock hushed and the newly arrived elder cleared his throat and spoke a bit louder.

"Mayor always claimed he was the son of a son of a son of a prophet. And what did he prophesy? He spent his entire time with this rookery telling us that the Coming would happen in his lifetime. He said he was duty-bound to impart all his knowledge to the Crow Corvus. Did it happen?"

137

"Why—no," someone said, with shocked awareness.

"No!" others called.

"No!" they shrilled in unison.

"No indeed!" the elder cawed. "Mayor was a wise old bird, a *strange* old bird with peculiar mannerisms and an alien way of speaking. He claimed he came from a country across the Gulf of Mexico. He talked about animals no one had ever seen, then or now. He was smart—oh he was that."

No one had ever spoken this way of Crow Mayor. The flock listened, dumbfounded.

"I'm not saying Mayor was bad," the elder laughed. "I'm not saying he didn't come from Mexico, either. He certainly had a peculiar mode of speech. But if he was a prophet, where was the Coming he always told us about? Where is the Crow Corvus?"

"He tricked us!" cried someone. Immediately the idea set in and the flock began to laugh. Crows have a deep appreciation for duplicity and wit. Nobody could take that away from the decedent. He'd tricked them—and kept up the ruse for years!

The elder spoke over his own chuckling, "So let's not get too excited if this yearling wants to be called *Mayor.* I personally think it is as fitting a name as any for a bird who thinks himself a prophet."

It was a good closing line. It brought the rookery down in gales of laughter. Hooting, the crowd slipped away even as Crow held his frozen, wings-out position of domination.

"Hey, Crow Mayor!" somebody teased. "Can I eat the farmer's corn, or will I sprout ears?"

Crow Mayor lowered his wings, his shoulders cramped from the awkward stance. He swallowed a rising lump in his craw.

"Gimme the weather forecast, hey, will you, Mayor?"

"When will the melons get ripe this year, Mayor?"

138

The laughter stabbed at Crow Mayor's heart, but he refused to retreat before their gibes and taunts.

When members of the flock addressed him thereafter, Crow found the name "Mayor" had a frivolity to it, like a worn joke that has lost significance except that it is universally known. In the weeks that followed, he suffered intermittent teasing when the flock was divided on an issue.

"Let's ask the prophet," someone would suggest. Then everyone would laugh before settling down to serious debate again.

The name was his. Now he must give it honor. He bore the gibes with apparent good nature. But deep inside, it hurt. The venerable name of Mayor had been reduced to a coarse joke. A lifetime of counseling, directing, and self-denial for the good of the flock—all gone. To fledglings hatched from this season forward, the name Mayor would be synonymous with charlatan.

It was the season for nest building and food was everywhere. A crow could take his choice of delicacies on any given day. Crops were sprouting, insects multiplying, fruits and berries were appearing on vine, shrub, and tree. As much as Crow had anticipated spring, it was different being a year old. It was the same as Crow remembered from nestling days, except now he knew that this opulent world of plenty was illusory. It was not a world assuring life to crows or any other creature. It was a world of food that would suddenly dwindle in early fall and disappear next winter. It was a world where delicious crawdads were toxic. It was a world of jeopardy, hardship, duress, and agony. It rightfully belonged to the fittest, and to the fittest it would go.

Observing the building of nests, mating, laying of eggs, and hatching, Crow was filled with an overwhelming sadness. If those fledglings knew what airways their wings must fly! The rookery was no place for a young male. The next few weeks belonged to mothers and their broods. The harried parents were busy stoking their fuel-burning tads with food. They had neither time nor the inclination to listen to Crow's repeated warnings.

"Get out of here!" a mother shrilled, suddenly attacking Crow Mayor. "Even if what you say is true, what can I do about it? Get away! I don't want my babies to hear such muck."

His message came softly, if at all, these days. They didn't want to hear it. Especially if it was true. Like Lotor and Adam, the flock cast the warnings out of their minds and ignored the bodies of fallen comrades. When the illness came upon any of them, they accepted it with stoic fatalism, expecting no pity and receiving none.

"Go away, Mayor," an elder advised quietly. "Nobody wants to hear your warnings. Be smart. Get out. You're making enemies that will last a lifetime. I'm telling you this for your own benefit. Go away."

He was no longer welcome anywhere in the rookery. His arrival was the signal for sneers and barbs; he was the butt of all jokes.

"Go," the elder repeated. "Be smart, young crow. Begone."

"Very well, elder."

"Good boy. Go now."

"All right, elder," Crow choked. "I'll go."

He stayed behind the outgoing flock the following morning and then, alone, departed in the opposite direction.

The elder observed this with sadness, but also with satisfaction. It wouldn't have been long before some irate parents attacked and hurt the erstwhile prophet. Better that he should go. And good riddance.

XV

"I'm trying!" Crow cried, his voice here, there, everywhere at once—unheard by any ears but his own. Entrancement does not allow communication except with another entranced being. The beasts, fish, and fowl did not know he was there. Nonetheless, Crow cried again, "I'm trying!"

Crow drifted to far valleys of distant continents, seeking imperiled creatures. Everywhere humans were multiplying. Their communities were like anthills, rising where conditions for life were most desirable. Wherever Crow looked, the human touch was on the land, spreading in every direction. Tilled fields, acrid fumes, dead rivers—this was their domain, littered with their trash.

There was no escaping man. Humans swarmed the earth oblivious to the fate of others, uncaring. Crow marveled at an intelligence that could build equipment to carry huge loads, and highways upon which to run such machinery. He was astounded at mountains they erected of steel, and their ability to cool the summer and warm the winter within such buildings. Awed, he examined structures built to fly faster than any bird—and carry many humans inside. The hum of humans, and human things, was a global drone unceasing and omnipresent.

Where there was man, all life except man himself became sparse or nonexistent. Crow saw jungles disappearing and highways snaking across virgin tropics. He saw wells pumping oil in remote deserts, oceans, and frozen tundras. Three thousand miles from any landfall, he found human debris floating in a scummy raft a mile long and a half a mile wide. Over entire nations hung an effluvium of noxious gases: fumes that seared lungs, scalded eyes, and dimmed the cleansing rays of the sun.

Ribbons of asphalt and concrete formed arteries, fed by thinner capillaries of intersecting roadways. Man moved with an ease that was the envy of migratory birds. They were intelligent creatures, these humans. Crow, during entrancement, observed men tunneling through water. What manner of magic was that? Elsewhere, man drew the water from a swamp and created high land out of low. At the same instant on another site, a concrete curve staunched a flow of water and a lake rose where none had existed before.

"I'm trying," Crow whispered to the universe. "I'm trying."

He awoke with the roar of his own pulse in his ears. He found himself in a storm, the wind shredding leaves from boughs and bending trees to the ground. Only his firmly clamped toes had kept his body in place. His feathers had been blown askew and every bent quill now made his flesh burn. A flock of displaced migrants was grounded nearby. Crow fought his way to their midst. To their surprise, the downed birds found a lone black figure shouting at them:

142

"We must adapt . . . change our habits . . . adapt to human ways . . . or die."

The soaked transients listened in a daze as Crow screamed above the hurricane, his caw a knell of doom in a tempest of wind.

"Where did he come from?" someone called.

"One of the locals," the reply.

"That crow needs codfish in his diet," a weary traveler commented.

Laughter in the face of disaster. Crow did not stop, reasoning with any creature willing to listen or incapable of avoiding him.

"Humans kill for sport, food, profit, fur, feathers—"

"Somebody peck that fool!"

"They cut forests, drain nesting areas—"

"Smack that dumb crow on the head and shut him up!"

"Because they fear bear, puma, 'gator—"

"Hey, Crow! Knock it off, will you?"

"Humans kill nuisance creatures, beaver, rabbit—"

"Look at that idiot crow. Hey! Beat it!"

"Kill to expand, build dams, power plants—"

"Get away from me, you zany bird! Get! Get! Get!"

"Kill by accident, pesticides, sprays—"

"That's enough, Crow. Go away now. Go on now."

"Adapt—only way—adapt or die!"

"I said get out of here, Crow. Now get away from here!"

"Poison streams, poison shellfish, poison—"

"Okay, birdie, we tried to tell you."

Whack! A crack on the skull. Whack! Another assailant joins. Whack! All over him now. Whack! Crow scrambled to the perimeter of soggy migrants and paused to shout a final word. Whack! Now they came at him in greater numbers. Whack! Whack! Whack!

Crow fled into driving sheets of rain, his plumage sodden and heavy. He was thrown against a tree and fell. Where he fell he lay without moving for several minutes, completely depleted, unable to rise.

He pulled himself leeward of the tree and shuddered, throwing off as much water as possible. He was cold, and yet the air was not all that cold. Lack of proper diet. Exhaustion. He needed sleep and food. Crow huddled next to the trunk, shivering. He did not feel well. He heard the grounded migrants trying to fly against the gale, only to thud down again. Crow closed his eyes, something he never did while on the ground. He teetered weakly and regained his equilibrium. Sleep. That's what he needed. Sleep and sustenance.

There in the whipping wind and rain, he slept and entranced anew.

His mind sought the winds circling the earth, the ones that had once borne him at such high speed. He found aerial routes that swirled, circled, sweeping the globe at breathless altitudes. From on high he saw the earth as a ball, green, blue, and swathed in white cumulus. From here, in his entrancement, it was only another step to go higher—farther—and farther out.

That pitiful orb, was it? That single speck in a dotted universe—that was *earth*? So insignificant, so puny beside her sister planets! Crow felt the ominous nothingness that is space. He moved at speeds where light stood still. Where was earth now? An infinitesimal germ in a swirling galaxy, a single piece of sand among tons of similar grains. Silence. The absolute lack of sound that makes the bodily functions a rumble, a pulse in the eardrums, the surge of blood—total silence!

Suddenly it frightened him to be here, there, expanding like cosmic gas, plummeting to the ends of the heavens.

Slowly, with great effort, he turned his mind, pulling himself back, snatching wisps of his being from outer space, drawing back to this one mote in the heap of celestial dust. Out of the void appeared earth. Out of the black came reflected light. Out of night came day. So beautiful, so green, so alive! Is it not true that any living thing is therefore necessarily dying? Crow pulled tendrils of his mind into a single all-seeing eye, scanning this grain of sand.

Save them? Which of them? Any of them? *How?* In this moment of entrancement, seeing everything reduced, nothing specific was important! What he did, if he did anything, must not be for crows alone, or armadillos, rattlesnakes, or raccoons. It must be for all inhabitants of this pitifully small globe. For indeed, from here, the problems of the world superseded any single issue. Did it not stand to reason, then, that from some point further out in space, the problem became galactic, not simply planetary?

"What can I do?" Crow cried to the galaxies winking reflective responses. "What can I do?"

From some stream of consciousness, in some remote corner of the world—or was it the galaxy?—the reply: Tell those who tell others.

"The thinkers?"

No. The travelers.

"The migrants!" Crow deduced. "Of course, tell the migrants! Tell them all, tell them until they believe the message."

His mind returned in fragments to the body lying rain-whipped and stone-cold at the foot of the tree which had provided his only shelter. Filtering particles of self, his being reaccumulated in this single feathered form.

Crow awoke slowly. Sound was the first conscious sensation. Still unmoving, he tried to identify the noises he heard, and could not. Gathering strength, he moved one toe. He was on

145

his side, his right wing caked with mud. The rain had stopped. The wind was gone. He roused himself, stiff in every joint. The grounded migrants were preening themselves into flight-shape. It was their flock talk he had not recognized a moment ago, a duck-like sound accentuated by rapidly clicking bills as they groomed themselves. Then, rising with thundering wing beats, hundreds of them trumpeted happily, turning west.

"What do you call yourselves?" Crow yelled.

"Blue geese," came the reply, and they were gone.

Crow rustled his soggy feathers, testing for flight. He rose with effort to a low limb and from there hop-stepped higher to a perch with a view. Meticulously, he took oil from his tail duct and reconditioned his quills. He sat fluffed like a ball, the sun drying away clammy moisture.

He perched there a long time, head turning in short, quick, typically passerine fashion, cocking this way and that with renewed alertness. Crow gazed across the marsh where the storm had caught him. The air was rain-washed and pure, temporarily cleansed of dust.

He spied a worm driven up by the rising water table. Crow dropped down and ate it. He had no trouble filling his craw. It was always good eating after a heavy downpour.

His hunger satisfied, Crow found a vantage point and there sat in solitary thought. He assessed his methods and found them wanting. He had tried to carry the message to many birds, but was getting nowhere. Even if he saw a hundred thousand birds, he would only have touched a tiny section of the globe. No, he had to do more than that. He sighed wearily. He knew now what he must do. If it took the balance of his life, he must try. He had to spread the message, and the migratory birds were his only hope.

146

*   *   *

Every incoming and outgoing flock of migrants found Crow there. He took the message to woodcock, whippoorwill, coot, and tern; bobwhite, night heron, teal, and kite; ibis, egret, duck, and grebe; osprey, eagle, owl, and hawk; birds of the black, blue, yellow, and red; meadowlark, oriole, redstart, buntings, sparrows, and dickcissel, all heard the message. Through fall, winter, and the summer that followed, he was there when the flights moved, his ebony body becoming so familiar that many who before had driven him away now tolerated his presence indifferently.

With the passing of another year, the reaction of the migratory birds altered perceptibly. They continued to talk among themselves, even as Crow spoke. They laughed, treating him as though he were simpleminded, snickering among themselves. He bored them.

"Come away, babies!" a mother would call. But now she didn't waste the energy it took to attack Crow.

"Oh, shoo, shoo!" one mother laughed. "Shoo away, funny bird! Don't pay any attention to the old crow, little ones. He's harmless."

Far removed from his own kind, Crow slept alone most nights, away from any flock and only rarely in the company of another crow. He deprived himself of sleep to seek out night migrants, and often neglected his need for fuel. On occasion, seeking a far place, he rose to the jet stream and flew to tell the message. The return trip sometimes took days or weeks. From first light to dusk, Crow worked with a single purpose of warning them all: adapt or die.

The seasons passed almost unnoticed. He learned to position himself farther south by winter, moving north in summer. The speed of the tropospheric winds carried him great

147

distances in a short time. It was always the homeward trek that left him exhausted, emaciated, barely able to move for several days until he regained weight and strength.

The disdain for Crow mounted with each passing year. He now found himself taunted even as he appeared before the arriving flocks.

"Well, well, well! Look who's here—the doom-doom bird!"

"Har! Har! Har! Tell us about the creepy-crawdads, Crow, old bird! Har, har, har!"

He suffered their abuse, verbal and physical. He was berated, assaulted, insulted. Those who had gone from hostility to indifference ultimately grew weary and drove him away again. Nevertheless, when new migrants appeared with each turn of the season, Crow was there to tell them.

He was hit with his first full molt, a debilitating experience that left him bedraggled and emotionally drained.

"What is that horrible-looking thing?" fledglings screamed at their elders.

"Really, Crow! Get out of here. Don't you crows know when it's poor taste to be in public?"

"Ugh! Double ugh! I'm going to be sick!"

"Go away, Crow. Good grief, did you see that molt? I've seen more feathers on a vulture's beak."

Crow reached birds from the Atlantic flyway to the east and the Mississippi flyway to the west. He met cedar waxwings from both coasts when they came through Alabama. Chimney swifts migrating two thousand miles to Peru were his unwilling audience as they paused before striking out across the Gulf of Mexico.

"Oh, no, not again!" they chorused. Moans rippled through the transitory flocks when Crow dropped down among them.

"Why won't you listen?" Crow demanded.

"Get out of here, birdie."

"Listen to my words!" Crow beseeched.

"We hear your words, old birdy, now go away."

"I'm trying—" Crow cried, lifting his voice over rude noises.

"Bllllpht!" someone honked.

"I'm trying to tell you—"

"Go fly into a tree, Crow! Get away from here!"

"I'm trying to tell you how to save yourselves!" Crow screamed.

Laughter. Hoots.

"Why?" Crow seethed. "Why don't you listen?"

Encouraged by the actions of their elders, several fledglings swooped at Crow, and he ducked defensively.

"Fools!" Crow shrilled. "Fools! All of you!"

"Tell me how to cure the chiggers, Crow!"

"Hey, hey, yeah, Crow! If you want to deliver us, deliver us from those itchy bugs, hey, hey! Whattayasay, Crow?"

"Har, har, har! A comic in black, that crow."

"I'm trying," Crow cried, taking wing as the fledglings nipped at his tail feathers. "I'm trying!"

He reasoned, argued, cajoled, and lamented—for what? They still ate what they'd always eaten. They flew the same flyways. As for himself, he was losing the bravest years of his life—those irreplaceable, vigorous years of his youth. He had met countless strangers and had not gained one new friend. His advice was unwanted, his presence unappreciated.

"Cawt! Cawt! Cawt!" he screamed. "Hello, world! My name's Crow Mayor. I am a fool!"

They spurned him, mocked him, pointed him out to nestlings, and his warnings fell on deaf ears. He had thought of nothing else; not one nest had he built for a mate of his own. Not one mate had he taken. He had spent his springs the same as his summers, falls, and winters: trying to tell them—Crow choked, a sickness rising in his breast—trying to *warn* them.

How long? How many springs? Seven? Could it have been seven years? During his quest to reach the migrants Crow had come to accept the ache in his wings from overuse, the emptiness of his craw from deprivation, the arthritic throb in his toes aggravated by hot desert floors and frozen snowscapes. For what? For what!

"Cawt! Cawt! Cawt!" he called, merely to hear his own voice.

"Go home, fool!" Crow told himself. "The world is the old world yet. Go home!"

XVI

Crow flew over patchwork parks in concrete cities, through a
grey haze of brackish air. On the horizon was the arc of the
Gulf, and this was his guide. Below him passed rust-red rivers
of clay-dyed waters churning south. To break the tedium of
his flight, he dipped, wheeled, and rested on a billowing
current of warm air. Then, at a steady two beats per second,
he regained the thirty-mile-per-hour speed he preferred. A
sudden and unexpected blast from a ship's horn made him
dart by reflex, then chuckle nervously at the false scare.

Once past areas of dense human habitation, he dropped
down, silent and watchful, to seek food and water. He paused
only briefly to replenish himself, then up again and homeward.

At last! Mobile Bay yawned ahead. Excitement rose in his
breast and with it came greater speed. Following the Tombigbee River, however, his ebullience dampened.

Houses stood where none had been before. He saw evidence of a fire, the woodland scorched, new growth thinly
emerging over charred earth. A recently constructed barn,
and there a bridge. A dirt road was now paved. Encroach-

ment. Steady, persistent, the approach of humans never faltered. Crow sighed deeply, wind-borne without effort, then continued with a steady wing beat.

A pecan grove had matured, the foliage now meshed, each tree touching another. Man-made ponds dotted the topography. Everywhere, things had changed. With vague instinct as his pilot and a few remaining landmarks to steer by, Crow sought the field that had been Dill's.

He found Dill's burrow abandoned, the mound eroded, the tunnel collapsed. Acreage once tended by humans was now a thicket of blackberry bramble. The weed-choked topsoil had been hardened by spates of rain and summer suns.

What would make the armadillos move? There had been no fire here. The natural growth was actually better for them than the human tillage had been. Armadillos cover several acres nightly, but they are not generally nomadic. It didn't appear they had been driven out by man, particularly since the field had been abandoned for agricultural purposes.

Crow flew over the area seeking evidence of a mound in progress. A subdued fear gripped him, a dread that made him ill. Circling outward to adjoining lands, he flew upward for a wider view. From clearing to clearing, checking every glen, Crow investigated each rise of soil with ascending hope and renewed disappointment. Where could they be!

That night Crow slept in the tree he had occupied years before when the armadillos kept watch while Crow, Lotor and Adam were entranced. His dreams were of days past and moments in the company of the armored foursome.

His subtle foreboding jelled during the night. Crow awoke with genuine apprehension for the safety of his friends. He saw these familiar fields as ominous places where death now lurked in every shadow.

He went in search of Adam. The rattlesnake had a predilection for high ground, shaded scrubland with a good stand of pines. He could be expected under or around fallen logs, rocky ledges, or coiled beneath the fanlike fronds of a palmetto.

Once more the alterations of man and time made it difficult for Crow to pinpoint the last place he'd met Adam. He soared as slowly as possible, frustrated by changes in the scene. Wasn't that the site where he'd last talked to Adam? No, there! Closer, studying. Or was it? Crow varied his altitude, hoping to regain a sense of perspective and dispel the confusion which muddled his mind.

In his quest, Crow failed to eat. The empty craw and worried mind combined to conjure vivid fantasies in which Crow imagined one terrible fate after another which might have befallen the armadillos and Adam. He spent that night tortured by dreams that awoke him with a jolt, cawing aloud. To escape this nightmare he remained awake, watching for the rising sun. While the trees were still dark etchings against barely distinguishable sky, Crow took off. To avoid the hazard of collision in flight, he rose half a thousand feet, flying as fast as he could, unseeing. He had but one thought now: find Lotor.

Surely the indomitable raccoon would still be there. If any creature could hold a domain and exist with human changes, it would be a raccoon. Fervently, Crow hoped it was so. If he could find Lotor, he was certain to locate the armadillos.

His mind was on Dill, his sight made nearly useless by the dimness of the predawn light. So deep was his distress at the transformations he had observed that Crow flew without thought to his movements. Blind to visual signs, his brain fogged with worry for his friends, he heard nothing.

Whoosh!

The hawk was on him without a sound. The first indication Crow had of danger was a mindless impulse that made him veer wildly. Instantly the predator wheeled, talons spread. Crow zigzagged groundward, seeking limbs, trees, bushes, anything to put between himself and death! Whoosh! Crow's back was grazed by needle-sharp claws and he felt the pluck of several feathers.

Crow dived straight at the ground, wings thrashing with all the forward drive he could muster. He knew he was sending himself to certain death when he hit at this velocity. There was no other option. The hawk was right behind him and Crow could visualize those rapier talons and hooked beak ready to stab and rip his flesh.

"Adapt!" he shrieked. "Adapt or die!"

Why did he shout that? Why that of all things?

His speed approaching fifty miles an hour, Crow did not pull up even as an inanimate shadow zoomed up at him.

"No!" he screamed. "No!"

He crashed into a dense, thorny bush, cringed, waited. Waited. Waited.

Breathless, heart hammering, Crow hung upside down without moving, aware that the phantom of death lurked overhead and was trying to relocate its prey. Crow dared not even draw together his outspread wings. He listened with the last iota of his ability and heard nothing but his own pounding heart.

For years he had deliberately placed himself in danger hundreds of times to deliver the message to birds of prey. He had been chased, pecked, driven to ground, but always in order to evict him. Never had anything attacked for the purpose of killing and devouring him.

As still as stone, Crow awaited the rising sun. Why hadn't the hawk followed through with his attack? Surely he had seen

Crow fall. The eyes of the predator were keen even in the half-light of predawn.

Crow lay with fear in every vein, ears ringing, waiting, waiting. As the sky paled from grey to ocher and blue, he dared to pull in first one wing, then the other. In spite of the hard use he'd made of his body, he was yet a young crow. His flesh and bones—a relatively small part of his apparent bulk— were strong and resilient. He had been impaled through several quills, but not a single briar pierced his flesh. He tried to right himself, to extricate his body from the spiked limbs. He slipped and fell, barely regaining his feet before hitting the ground.

He crouched there, looking up through backlighted boughs, blinded by the first rays of dawn. Gingerly he tested his wings, hopping out from under the bush that had saved him. His muscles ached as though the sinews had been sprinkled with grit, every move abrasive to tendon and bone. He worked his wings forward, back, then stretched to relieve kinks caused by remaining so long in one position. Nothing broken, miraculously, nothing cracked. He cocked his head, carefully studying the trees above him. The bright light of the morning sky made it impossible to see. Any clump of leaves could be the hawk.

"Oh," Crow moaned. "Oh." His breast constricted; he was shaking. "Oh," he said again, the quaking now racking him to his toes. He swallowed, swallowed again, then ejected stones in his craw.

"Jake! Jake! Jake!" A bluejay's penetrating cry made Crow jump. As the distant cousin flew over, Crow ducked defensively, wingtips touching soil.

He tried to fly—and plummeted into dense undergrowth. Nausea made him stick out his tongue, beak agape, but there was nothing more to give. "Oh," he whispered. There he stayed, long into the morning, shivering, ill from shock, struggling to comprehend why he was still alive.

Finally he gained a low perch and from there, in short flights, attained a branch where he felt more secure. Even after the bill-rattling tremors subsided, Crow still dodged shadows and recoiled at sudden noises. Taking deep draughts of air, he struggled to resurrect his composure, to rein in his nerves. Still shaky, he took off at treetop level, heading for Lotor's range.

Without spirit, his observations now mechanical, Crow noted the continuing signs of change. A shopping center where once there had been a swampy bog. Culverts channeled water which could no longer seep underground. In place of trees were incandescent lights on creosote poles. Flat graveled roofs reflected sunlight and the hum of air conditioners came to Crow's ears.

Huddled like metallic ants, automobiles clustered in geometric patterns, each carefully placed between fish-rib lines crisscrossing black asphalt. Sparrows, the ubiquitous avians which most benefited from man's structures, mingled with pigeons amid human feet on the sidewalks. Crow passed in silence, not wishing to risk another confrontation.

Beyond the shopping center were human dens, quilted lawns, skinny trees to replace those uprooted by builders. Cats and dogs were everywhere, guaranteeing continual harassment for every wild thing. There! Ahead! The remnants of marshland.

Something was missing even here, where humans had halted their construction. It took several minutes of careful examination for Crow to realize what was gone. The moss! Long wispy fingers of vegetation which had always draped the trees now dwindled to nothing. Had humans somehow managed to kill the air-feeding moss, too?

Crow was struck with the absence of feral sounds. Gone were the barely perceptible noises created in any natural woodland. The cough of a bobcat, the chattering of squirrels, the tapping of woodpeckers, the music of the wild—now mute. Here in the shadow of human habitation, all survivors remained silent.

"Cawt! Cawt! Cawt!" Crow screamed. There was no response. In the distance, Crow heard a rumbling diesel, the shriek of a factory whistle.

He descended on the tallest of several dead trees. It was the kind Lotor preferred for a den. Crow analyzed the surroundings. There was no longer a running creek. The marsh was bounded on one side by human homes, on another by the shopping center. The yelp of a dog was clearly audible not far distant. Lotor would not be here!

But then Crow noted fresh scratches and telltale hairs around a hole below him.

"Lotor!" Crow called. "Lotor!"

Crow dropped to a lower branch. "Lotor, are you there?"

A faint rustling reached Crow's ears. He called again, "Lotor! Hello, Lotor!" A masked face appeared at the portal, eyes squinted against the glare, moist nose sniffing the air.

"Lotor, is that you?"

Now the entire head poked out and the sleepy raccoon peered at the intruder.

"Lotor?"

"Crow?" Lotor answered hoarsely.

Crow laughed.

"Crow!" Lotor squealed, blinking fast to throw off a veil of somnolence. "Crow! Is it really you?"

XVII

"Wait a minute, I've gotta—" The raccoon pushed through the hole of his den. "I've gotta enlarge this thing," he grumped, wedged half out. "Hold on a—get my leg through the—Crow, I think I'm stuck! No, no, wait a minute now. Here we go, my leg's asleep. I need to gnaw this thing out a bit, but in the winter it cuts down on drafts and—yep, I'm gonna make it now. Hold on! Here we go. Here we go!"

Slowly, the burly raccoon's body ballooned from the aperture. He clawed for leverage, pushing with his back legs, teeth bared in a grimace. He exhaled to make himself smaller.

"About got it now," Lotor puffed. "If I can pull this—there!" He snatched free and let himself down to Crow's limb.

"One of these days I'm going to get stuck in there," Lotor panted. "I've considered moving, but housing being what it is these days, you have to fight for a decent den. Maybe I'm getting soft with old age, but it doesn't seem fair to dislodge a tenant simply because I'm big enough or mean enough to do it. Know what I mean?"

"I do, Lotor."

"Oh, Crow," Lotor wheezed, "it's good to see you!"

"Apparently life has been abundant for you, Lotor."

"Abundant?" Lotor queried. "Oh, you mean my weight. Yes, well, humans exist on diets fraught with starches, and I eat what humans eat these days."

"You do?"

"I didn't have much of an option," Lotor said. "They dried up the creek and paved most of my territory. Remember what you said, 'adapt or die'? I adapted. But I get satisfaction in small ways," Lotor chuckled. "I raid their garbage cans, chase cats up drainspouts, and give their dogs apoplexy. I rattle those garbage cans before the break of dawn, the lights come on, and humans scream at the dogs."

"So you adapted," Crow said, redirecting the conversation.

"I did indeed! You were right about adapt or die. Those that didn't, like Dill and Adam—"

Crow's gasp halted Lotor. "You didn't know?" Lotor asked, softly.

"No."

"I'm sorry, Crow. I assumed you knew. Adam was caught by humans surveying the area. If Adam hadn't rattled, chances are he wouldn't have been seen. You remember the trouble he had controlling that tail of his. Anyway, they found him."

"Oh," Crow whispered.

"They killed Adam and walked around holding him up by the tail, showing—" Lotor paused. "Humans don't leave any dignity, you know."

"Oh, Lotor!"

"They cut off his rattles, Crow. All those years, Adam would have gladly given them up. Then after he's dead they cut them off."

"Oh, no, Lotor," Crow said.

159

After a pensive silence, Lotor added in a low voice, "They got Dill, too."

"All of them?" Crow cried.

"One was run over by an automobile," Lotor related. "Dill was so nearsighted I guess he didn't see it coming. One got trapped by a human. We never saw him again. One died from drinking bad water. I warned him about sewers, but he wouldn't listen. They weren't the same after the first one got hit by the car. . . . The last one was shot."

"For food?"

"For nothing," Lotor said, his tone even. "We were over at a new dump the humans built. A human was shooting cans and bottles. He saw Dill and—"

Crow's eyes closed tightly.

"I'm sorry, Crow."

"Couldn't they *sense* that Adam and Dill were thinkers?"

"Evidently humans don't rely on sense too much," Lotor concluded. The raccoon's tone changed. "Well, look at my friend Crow! How's it been with you?"

"I've been a fool, Lotor."

Lotor grunted. "Join the largest fraternal disorganization in the world, Crow." He scratched one underleg with the opposite forefoot, his coat shifting loosely with the effort.

"I've gone from one end of this country to the other," Crow said, "making a joke of myself."

The portly raccoon gazed at Crow steadily.

"Wasted my time," Crow said, his tone dropping. "Wasted my youth."

"I'm sorry, Crow."

"You were right, Lotor. It was hopeless."

Lotor backed down the tree, attempting to see past his prominent hips as he slid groundward. "Come on, Crow," the raccoon offered. "You need something to lift your spirits.

Your arrival, as it happens, has come at precisely the right moment. The scuppernongs are fermenting."

"Fermenting?"

"They're good when they're ripe," Lotor said, "but at this point they're something else again! I've spent the last few days testing them. Today they should be excellent."

Crow trailed the ambling raccoon in short hops, moving from bush to shrub above him. In some respects Lotor was unchanged. He still loved to talk, and there was no hurrying him.

Lotor halted at the base of a towering hardwood tree. "Say, Crow, check that hole up there, will you? I've been meaning to look that over. There've been some bees around this tree. I didn't want to climb all the way up there on a hunch. No, no, higher! Right there, see it?"

"It's a beehive all right," Crow reported.

"Ah!" Lotor said. "Take a look inside, Crow, and see if they're still active. They should be settling down this time of year."

"Lotor, I don't believe I want to stick my head in a beehive."

"Oh." Disappointment. "Well, I'll check it some other time."

Lotor still couldn't pass a rock without turning it, or a hole without poking it. His conversation never lagged; he commented on anything that came to mind, all the while investigating this and that.

"Humans chain their dogs," Lotor said. "Stupid beasts, dogs."

"I wouldn't know," Crow said, "never having made contact with a dog."

"If you want to see a dog go berserk," Lotor commented, "steal his water bowl. I stand beyond the end of his chain playing with that bowl, and here he comes—wham! Hits the end of that chain and nearly turns himself inside out. I've seen them gnash their teeth, froth at the mouth, eyes bulging, barely able to breathe. So what does he do? Back to the doghouse and here he comes again. Wham! It's a wonder it doesn't break his neck."

"I wouldn't know," Crow said.

"Humans look after those dogs, though! You wouldn't believe how they feed them," Lotor said. "Now if you *really* want to see a dog go insane, snatch his food. He couldn't eat another bite if you force-fed him, but he'll rearrange every bone in his spine trying to get it back."

"What if the chain broke?" Crow inquired.

"It won't."

"What if it did?" Crow persisted.

"Well," Lotor said amiably, "I guess I'd have to whip me a mongrel. Turn this way, Crow. The vine is over here."

Lotor paused to crack a nut between his teeth. "Want a nut, Crow?"

"No thanks."

"Lousy nuts," Lotor muttered. "I've been spoiled by thin-shelled pecans."

"Lotor, how much farther to the scuppernongs?" Crow urged, hoping to hurry their progress.

"Not far." Crunch! Another nut. "Really lousy," Lotor said, his tongue fishing for a shell fragment under one lip.

"Shall I go ahead and wait for you?" Crow asked pointedly.

"No, no, I'm coming. You still on the crawdad wagon, Crow?"

Exasperated, Crow said, "Lotor, you're confusing me with strange idioms! What wagon are you talking about?"

"Sorry," Lotor said. "Vernacular of the day. I suppose humans are rubbing off on me. You're still not eating crawdads?"

162

"Please, Lotor," Crow said, his irritation now overt, "confine your thoughts to literal terms. You're using words that in no way apply to what you're saying."

"Sorry, Crow. It's a weakness."

At last, after several more false starts and lengthy halts, they reached the holly tree. A rich aroma of rotting fruit assailed Crow's nostrils.

"Forget those on the vine," Lotor advised. "The ones on the ground are choice."

The odor itself was intoxicating. Crow pecked one of the thick-skinned grapes and found it delicious! In short order, both Lotor and Crow attained a state of being which the raccoon referred to as "a terpsichorean trip of the first magnitude." The phrase was utterly meaningless to Crow, but he didn't trouble himself about it.

"Ever see a chihuahua, Crow?"

"Nope, don' believe so."

"Something like a rat, but's a dog," Lotor said, resting on his coccyx, surrounded by scuppernong hulls. "Don' do credit to rats or dogs, s'far's I can tell."

"Never saw one."

"Din' miss much."

"What was that, Lotor?"

"What was what, Crow?"

"What was that sound?"

"What sound?"

"*That* sound."

"Oh. 'Scuse. Was a hiccup, Crow."

"What kinda cup?"

"*Hick*-cup. 'Scuse again. Contractions of the diaphragm," Lotor said.

"I'm stuffed," Crow said.

"How d'ya feel?" Lotor inquired.

"Stupor!"

"Lemme hear that again, Crow."

"Stupor!" They both burst into laughter.

"I cad ebben think ennymore," Crow said.

Lotor had pulled his tail up between his legs, sitting propped against the tree, peering intensely at the ringed appendage, picking out beggar's lice. His tongue protruded slightly. Finally he threw the tail away as though for the last time. "Can't see 'em anyhow, so why mess with it?"

"You're fat, Lotor."

"Don' be unpleasant, Crow. Nothing's worse'n a sour pickled crow." That struck Lotor as hilarious and he rolled over on his side, repeating, "Sour pickled crow!" His mirth gained the better of him and he lay chuckling, plump body jiggling.

"This business of fermenting's not s'bad," Crow said.

"What some more?" Lotor asked.

"No."

"One or two more?"

"No, no."

"Well. I'm sleepy. G'night."

"Wade a minute, Lotor! I can't sleep here. I'd end up been something t'eat."

"Lemme hear that again, Crow."

"Something t'eat, Lotor. Hungry looking for something t'eat."

Lotor hiccuped and giggled, the two of them repeating "sour pickled crow" and "something t'eat," renewing the laughter over and over.

Lotor curled up in a nest of scuppernong rinds and Crow huddled next to the furry form. There they drifted off to sleep. It was the slumber of a nestling—dreamless, uncaring, unburdened. Late that night, Lotor the nocturnal awoke briefly. He consumed more scuppernongs and returned to Crow's side.

"Crow," Lotor whispered.

"Hmm?"

"I'm glad you're back, Crow."

"Hmm."

Lotor sighed and closed his eyes.

XVIII

Among cardboard cartons and discarded cans, in the daily trash behind the stores of the shopping center, Lotor introduced Crow to an abundant supply of edibles. Their only competitors were rodents, which Lotor now ignored outright, and an occasional stray pet from nearby neighborhoods. Hunger was quickly satisfied; food was no longer a primary concern. At the first pang, they had only to make the short trek to the shopping center and help themselves.

They spent many hours of each day following idle pursuits, fearing nothing, eating, sleeping, talking. Crow should have been as content as the burly raccoon. Then why, Crow wondered, was he so restless?

True, they had more food than they could ever consume, served to them daily in the debris from the human markets. They need have no fear of predators—what creature would risk battle when the feast was available to all and required no conflict to win it?

Nonetheless, the pattern of their lives disturbed Crow. Like the sixth sense that warned of lurking danger, Crow's vague discontent would not be allayed. With growing awareness, he faced the reality of this world Lotor called home.

The natural, constantly evolving, and never-ending cycle of food was gone. The source now, the sole source, was the tempting larder of the human waste piles. On this banquet they were growing fat and ever more dependent. Their bodies had become so accustomed to easy living that their muscles were soft and quick to tire. Were their eyes as keen as once they had been? Did they listen on these uneventful nights for the danger that once preyed on the unsuspecting?

The creeks of minnows and the muddy homes of crawdads, the marshy habitat of earthworms and emerging larvae were now packed and dried. No longer were juicy grubs burrowing in rotted limbs and fallen trees; the woodland had been denuded long ago. The tilled fields and seasonal crops had given way to homes and streets and potted plants. Most of the brambles of blackberry and other wild fruit had been pruned out of existence.

Any attempt to discuss these observations with Lotor left the normally talkative raccoon surly and silent.

"Let's move, Lotor," Crow urged.

"Move?" Lotor balked. "Why?"

"There's nothing here anymore, Lotor, except humans and things which belong to them."

"Crow," Lotor said, amazed, "this is the good life! We sleep securely, want for nothing. What more could you ask?"

"Perhaps we are not as secure as we feel, Lotor."

"Chiggers, Crow! We eat, we grow fat."

"Perhaps too fat, Lotor."

"So what?" Lotor questioned.

"It isn't natural," Crow persisted.

"Listen, Crow," Lotor said, amiably, "you're doing all right

167

on the same diet. Your feathers are shining, your craw is full."

"What happens if the food supply changes, Lotor?"

"Since when has food been assured, Crow? Anywhere! Did you ever see crawdads jump up into your beak?"

"When crawdads are scarce, I hunt other things," Crow said.

"If the shopping center closes," Lotor agreed, "I'll hunt elsewhere. Until then, life couldn't be better. Did you get any of those grapes they threw away yesterday?"

"The point is," Crow persisted, "I don't think you would be able to hunt anymore, Lotor."

Lotor considered this a moment. "I'll worry about that when it happens," he concluded.

"Look what's happening to us, Lotor! We're sluggish, soft, acting as though there is no peril in life."

"Now, Crow, don't get wound up on your doomsday stuff."

"Look at yourself, Lotor," Crow said. "You're being domesticated. Like a cow or a horse—or a dog."

"Are you trying to insult me, friend Crow?" Lotor asked, without rancor.

"I'm trying to make you see life as it is, Lotor. Face reality!"

"Reality?" Lotor scoffed. "Let me give you the reality of the situation, Crow. You say I'm like a cow or a horse or a dog? There's a big difference. The cow is fed by man in return for its milk and or meat. The horse is to be ridden or worked. The dog lives at the end of a chain. I don't give, Crow. I *take*.

"When humans started paving my territory, I quaked with terror, scared I'd starve to death. They dried up my creek, sprayed for bugs, and put a film of oil on the only remaining water, to kill mosquito larvae. I holed up in my den for weeks with the tree shaking from pile drivers. Then I faced reality, Crow.

"My creek was gone. But there's water aplenty in every

168

backyard and concrete culvert. Also gone are the mosquitoes, and the spraying did away with most ticks and lice, too. At one time I scrounged from sunset to sunrise to exist and some days did without altogether. I can remember times when an insect appetizer was the main course.

"Not anymore, Crow. Now I amble over to the shopping center and help myself to what I want. I can afford to be finicky about it, too. It beats algae and ants for dinner. Winter, spring, summer, and fall, there's always a supply of food now.

"Maybe you've forgotten the shotguns and hunting dogs. They came to kill, Crow. These city humans don't hunt. Not once have I been treed by a dog since they built all those houses you see out there. Not one gunshot have I heard.

"These humans are a different breed of man, Crow. They don't want my hide; they don't need me to eat. Other humans killed everything that displeased them. These humans don't seem displeased to share their garbage with me. All my fears of hunger are gone. All right, I'm fat and soft. If I'm supposed to deprive myself now that I have it so good, forget it! And I'll thank you not to get insulting about it."

"You know what that makes you, Lotor?" Crow asked, his incensed attitude surprising even himself. "That makes you weak. You aren't wild anymore."

"You preach a lot, Crow," Lotor snapped. "Why don't you practice what you preach?"

"What does that mean?" Crow asked.

"You spent your youth chasing flock after flock, telling them, 'adapt or die.' Very well, now I have adapted. You counseled wisely, Crow. I listened."

"No you didn't, Lotor. You took the line of least resistance. You've done that from the outset. This 'good life' you speak of was none of your doing. You were cowering in your den, and no action on your part brought about your salvation."

"Crow, you're a pain in the hindsight, do you know that? If your message is so important, why did you come home and stop preaching it?"

"Damn you, Lotor!"

"And damned I may be, Crow. How about you? You went out to warn the world, and how much good did it do?"

"They wouldn't listen!" Crow said sharply. "I needed help. I came to you and Adam. Oh, no! Neither of you would try. You stuck your head in a hole and your tail between your legs and insisted it was hopeless."

"Wasn't it?" Lotor countered.

"All right, Lotor, all right! You buried your head and survived. Your head is still buried. But hope that nothing happens to the shopping center, Lotor. You couldn't shift for yourself if your life depended on it. And your life *would* depend on it."

"Crow, have any living creatures changed because of your efforts?"

No reply.

"I use humans as a source of food, Crow. I had no choice. They destroyed my territory. I did as you suggested; I adapted. Can you tell me any other creature anywhere that followed your counsel?"

"No."

"Have you stopped to consider why?" Lotor asked.

"Yes." Crow was trembling with anger born of frustration. "I shouted. I screamed. The fools—"

"Crow," Lotor's tone lowered, "You're always offering cardinal rules. Now let me give you one: for a whisper, the ear comes nearer."

Stunned, Crow peered at Lotor's masked face framed in the hole of the raccoon's den.

170

"Crow, only those who want to believe will flock to a preacher, but every listener loves a teller of tales."

"Of course," Crow marveled. "Teach, don't preach. Parables teach more than canons."

"Not that any creature wants to hear that same tired message, Crow."

"I went at it all wrong," Crow said, his tone rising.

"Crow! Are you suggesting that you might go out to seek unwilling audiences again?"

"Yes, Lotor! Yes, and thank you!"

"I think you're part woodpecker, Crow."

"Why?"

"You seem to enjoy knocking your head against a tree."

Leaving at dawn as the raccoon settled into his den to sleep away the day, Crow flew toward the resting grounds of migratory birds passing through the area. He approached his task with less naïveté than before. Years of abuse, castigation, and expulsion tempered his mood, altered his tone, and gave him more restraint.

His approach more docile, Crow no longer shouted his warnings, demanding attention. Now he lured the aliens into conversational exchanges.

And he told them stories.

He told tales of wonders they'd never seen, of death and danger, triumphant quests, and comic blunderings. For those who sang, he wove stories into song. Every story, every song, contained a deadly serious point to ponder. He told them of the Coming. His tales revolved around a wise raccoon, a stubborn crow, a nervous rattlesnake, and a loyal chorus of armadillos.

When the laughter subsided, when the reveries were done—they remembered. Thus, he taught.

"Do you fear predators?" Crow would ask.

"Of course!"

"Human progress is a predator," Crow taught. "It consumes our nesting grounds, forces us to change breeding areas, alters our feeding habits. As you are wary of the hawk, so be alert to man's encroachment. You would not willingly die for the hawk, neither should you succumb to human changes which ultimately bring doom."

"What can we do?"

"Adapt," Crow whispered.

"Adapt?" they asked, bewildered.

"Move your breeding grounds, alter your flyways, seek new feeding areas. Adapt. Therein lies survival."

From continent to continent the message was borne. Sooty shearwater and wheatear, birds of the black, blue, red, and yellow, first laughed, later became thoughtful; ibis and egret, grebe and duck, warblers and waxwings all had cause to consider the disappearing marsh, paved prairies, denuded forests, and redirected rivers. Kingfisher, coot, bobwhite, and kite, vireo, meadowlark, oriole, and redstart, all paused at some point in their existence to remember what the crow had been saying.

Gulls told petrels and petrels the terns and terns the teals and teals told sandpipers. From sea birds to shore walkers, to sand dwellers and inland flocks, the word passed. From Alabama to the Arctic Circle and on to the African veldt, from jungled tropics to mountain heights, the message was heard. From crumbling cliffs to frozen tundra, woodcock to whippoorwill, osprey to hawk and to the eagle's lofty retreat, they repeated what he had said. First with ridicule, then with sober reflection, two billion winged messengers carried Crow's pronouncements. They had berated and abused him, taunted and teased; but they did not forget.

Insecticide-infested insect-eaters settled on calcium-depleted eggs and a crunch of shell reminded them. They stared at the aborted life, and Crow's admonishments returned to haunt them.

Blue geese, ducks, and waterfowl followed ancient migratory flyways and arrived to find parched earth where once cattails and hyacinth grew. They remembered.

A Peruvian condor soared above Andean canyons and a shot sent the vulture fluttering groundward. Too late remembered.

Pelicans with pasted plumage settled on oil slicks, and there floundered and died, remembering.

Pink-plumed flamingos under close human guard cursed their progenitors and clung to an existence which, once gone, would be the end of their species.

Plovers in Scotland bluffs, curlews in Tahiti, the cuckoo of New Zealand, returning to ancestral homes now destroyed, circled, confused—and remembered.

They had laughed, observed, finally learned at dear cost, pondered their losses, and later remembered the solitary crow with the ominous omens and ready advice.

It took twenty-five generations! Twenty-five seasons of nest building, of incubation, of surviving fledglings, before the last titter faded, the ultimate snicker died. Then Crow wasn't funny anymore.

Young ones grew older, elders reflected, cardinal rules were repeated, and everywhere the survivors—remembered.

Obesity and overabundance of food had robbed Lotor of several traits essential for existence in the wild. Sluggish in movement, he remained supremely confident in his freedom, the honed edge of his awareness dulled. Waddling through the macadam alleys of civilization, Lotor quickly filled his belly but not his time. He would then make tours of neighborhood garbage cans, but this perfunctory chore was more for curiosity than for need of edibles, and still Lotor had many hours before Crow would awaken. That left only mischief.

Now and then he chanced upon a dog or cat running loose, but a good nip on the snout sent these creatures on their way. No one domestic dog is a match for a fully grown raccoon. Therefore Lotor moved with impunity through the backyards and outbuildings.

His favorite diversion was a mongrel dog which was part shepherd and other parts unknown. This hapless animal was securely chained to one corner of a house, which did nothing to improve his disposition. The house was enclosed by a wood fence with an inner border of flowers. The humans had carefully tethered the dog so that he couldn't reach the plants. It was in this zone of safety which Lotor walked, ostentatiously ignoring the infuriated beast straining to reach him.

"Er-er-er-er-er-er." Chirping with anticipatory pleasure, Lotor squeezed through a hole in the fence and hugged the wall encircling the yard.

"Rowr, rowr, rowr!" Whang! The chain reached its limit and the dog's hindmost quarter bypassed his front as his momentum came to an abrupt halt.

"Rowr, rowr, rowr!"

The snapping fangs a scant two feet away, Lotor moved with nonchalance toward his objective: a birdbath in which there was always fresh water.

"Er-er-er-er-er." Lotor's chuckles only served to madden the mongrel all the more.

"Rowr, rowr, rowr!"

Lotor reached the birdbath and scaled it, his weight almost

tipping the ceramic fixture as he pulled himself up. Now atop the bath, his ringed tail hanging over one side, he cleansed both forefeet, drank his fill, and washed his whiskers.

"Rowr, rowr, rowr!"

"Shut up!" A human voice. "Hyar! Shut up, dog!"

"Rowr, rowr, rowr!"

"What is it, Henry?"

"A cat I think. Hyar, shut up, dog!"

"Really, Henry, he'll wake the dead."

"Rowr, rowr, rowr!"

Time to go. Lotor eased himself down, hanging by his front feet a second before dropping the last few inches to the ground.

"Every night!" the human female lamented.

"Rowr, rowr, rowr!"

Lotor was against the wall now, pushing through flowers and shrubs, casually making his way back to the exit.

His only warning was a dull snap. The human, disgusted with these nocturnal disturbances, released the dog.

"Sic!"

The mongrel pinned Lotor with a bound, catching the raccoon completely off guard. The canine's fangs closed on Lotor's back with a sickening crunch of flesh and bone. Hissing, spitting, snarling, the two animals rolled as Lotor tried to shake the beast away, clawing for freedom.

"Sic, boy, hyar, get him!"

"Henry? What's going on out there? Henry!"

"Get him, boy!"

Seized by primordial instinct, enraged by months of teasing from Lotor, the dog reveled in his surprise assault. He shook Lotor viciously, fangs ripping.

"Henry! Is that the cat from next door?"

The human grabbed his dog. He couldn't allow the neighbor's cat to be slain.

175

"That's enough, boy! Here, let go! Let go!"

Gasping, frothing, the snarling dog's jaws relaxed and Lotor tore free.

"Hey! That's no cat!"

Instantly the dog was at Lotor again, but this time the raccoon wheeled and returned as good as he got. With a yelp, the dog withdrew a second, one eye slashed. Lotor dived for the hole.

He would have made it if he'd been four pounds lighter. His hair and loose pelt snagged for only a moment, but during that fleeting instant the dog's fangs snapped a hind leg, and Lotor shrilled in agony as the bone broke. He snatched free as fur and flesh were rent. Hobbling, dragging the useless appendage, Lotor sought safety.

Now it seemed that every dog in the area was around him, snarling, the yelps and barks splitting the night as Lotor passed the fence, tether, or window which held back potential attackers.

Hurry! He turned a corner, the bumping leg making him whirl with fresh pain, snapping at foes no longer there—it was his own leg he bit. Hurry! Hurry! Lotor scrambled up a low wall, hung precariously a moment, and lost his footing, crashing back. He gasped, searing pain shooting from the leg. He gathered his last ounce of strength and tried again, leaping, clawing, crying, up—and over.

"Crow!"

Crow's eyes opened to dark. His ears rang with a sudden adrenal flow.

"Crow!" Screeching.

"Lotor, is that you?"

"Down—below. Oh, Crow!"

"I can't see you!" Crow cried. "What's wrong?" A whimper-

176

ing, the sound of nails scratching to climb the tree, then slipping back.

"Lotor? What's wrong?"

"Yeee!" Lotor's scream pierced Crow's ears.

"Lotor, answer me! Lotor! What's wrong?"

Gasping, panting, a groan.

More calmly, holding his tone to an even level, Crow asked anew, "Lotor, what's wrong? Tell me."

"Dog—dog—got me, Crow. Stupid dog—oh, Crow!"

Crow's eyes were as wide as possible, straining to see what he knew he would not be able to see in the dark.

"Easy, Lotor. Easy. It isn't long until dawn."

At daybreak, Crow dropped down beside Lotor. His gums white from shock and loss of blood, Lotor lay at the base of his tree, each panted breath gurgling. A mortal patina glazed the raccoon's eyes. He ebbed from feverish babbling to coma, only to awaken, teeth gnashing, a red froth in the corners of his mouth.

"Steady, Lotor," Crow soothed, his tone smooth, covering tormented frustration.

Once Lotor came up screaming and viciously attacked the source of greatest pain, his dangling leg. Horrified, Crow watched the raccoon chew it off and fall back spent.

Words his only balm, Crow struggled to suppress his own misery and transmit comforting thoughts to the tortured creature. Death, the ultimate mercy, was slow coming.

"We were rare, Crow," Lotor gasped.

"That we were, Lotor."

"What—" Lotor closed his eyes tightly. "What a waste!"

"Lie back, Lotor. Try to rest."

"I was young, Crow," Lotor cried. "I should've helped."

Moments passed in which Crow could not fathom the thoughts that jumbled in the raccoon's mind. Then Lotor mumbled, "Early wise and late to reason."

"We all were," Crow said.

"Lie."

"No, it's true."

"Lie," Lotor repeated, and succumbed to unconsciousness.

Through all of the daylight hours and into another night, Lotor suffered. He saw things that were not there. He refought his battle with the dog. He cursed his stupidity and indolence. Then, when the nerves could stand pain no longer, Lotor drifted into a semiconscious twilight where he spoke softly, his thoughts much as he'd always talked.

"Did you ever look in a human house, Crow?"

"No, Lotor, I never did."

"They make it rain."

"Rain? In the house?"

Crow waited, waited, thinking the raccoon had slipped into another period of sleep. Then, a voice in the dark, Lotor spoke again. "I heard water running and climbed up to see. Female human—head in a sack—in a shower-bath; bathing. She—she saw me."

With an aching heart, Crow responded. "What did she do?"

"She bumped the tub."

"Bumped the tub?"

"With a piece of cloth in front of her. Bumped the tub. Here. There. Screaming. A man came in and she pointed at me, told him I had—a mask on."

A long pause, only Lotor's shallow breathing.

"I left," Lotor concluded.

"That was probably wise," Crow suggested.

"Yes. Wise. Early wise, late to season."

"You were always wise, Lotor."

Lotor coughed, his breathing progressively more labored. "I watched, Crow—" Long pause. "When humans came to see the window—where I looked in—they found tracks, knew it was a—a raccoon."

Crow waited.

"They said—the female human said—'It was almost human,' and they all laughed at her. You know what that means, Crow?"

"What what means, Lotor?"

" 'Almost human.' "

"No, what does it mean?"

"It—it's no compliment, Crow."

XIX

The southern crow appeared in a Pennsylvania rookery. He was large, seasoned, the youthfulness of his plumage deceptive to strangers. He spoke in soft tones, his voice carrying a peculiar quality that evoked thoughtful response. They soon learned of his wisdom, and to this elder even the eldest turned for advice. He earned their respect with his counsel. He received their admiration for his compassion. He awed them with stories of places and animals such as none of them had ever seen. He held them enthralled with tales of things beyond their comprehension. He told them of the Coming.

"Elder?"—a young voice in the night.

"Yes, fledgling?"

"Tell us again, elder."

"Tell you what?" He knew what.

"About Crow Corvus, elder. About the Coming."

The elder sighed, head pulled between his shoulders, eyes closed.

"He was the son of a son of a son of a prophet," the elder

spoke by rote. "He died and was reborn. He was Crow Corvus. He made friends with armadillos, a kind of animal found far south of here. They were simple animals and it took four to make a single mind. From them, Crow Corvus learned of simple love. He loved the armadillos."

His voice was a drone in the dark; the rookery sat hushed, listening. "Crow Corvus communicated with a rattlesnake, and the serpent filled him with distrust. Crow Corvus wanted to overcome his suspicion and could not; from this he learned to tolerate weakness in others. He came to love the reptile and was grieved that he had learned so late."

The rookery stirred, and the elder waited for silence.

"He was befriended by a raccoon, and the raccoon was named 'Lotor.' Lotor taught Crow Corvus about visions and made Crow Corvus see the world as it was. From the raccoon, Crow Corvus gained both knowledge and wisdom.

"In a vision, Crow Corvus saw many dangers. He saw the threat to all living things. He went forth to warn the creatures of the world, and he was rejected. His own rookery exiled him and birds of many feathers ridiculed him. He was disheartened and sick with his failure. The raccoon was wise. He taught Crow Corvus the wisdom of restraint. With the strength of experience and maturity, Crow Corvus began anew. For generations he carried the message—adapt or die.

"Those who listened, survived. Those who did not were doomed."

After a long silence, a lone, sleepy voice asked what everyone already knew. "You flew with Crow Corvus, elder?"

"Yes, fledgling, I did."

"He was your friend?"

"He was a friend to every living thing."

"Even humans?"

"Even humans, fledgling. Go to sleep now."

181

"And you were there when he died?"

"I was."

"How did he die?"

"At the hands of time, fledgling. He had served his purpose. Go to sleep. We're going to a melon field in the morning."

"Yes, elder."

The elder sidestepped to a more comfortable position for his arthritic feet. Somewhere in the rookery a brief squabble erupted among yearlings; the flock shifted, settled.

He clamped his toes securely. A final stretch of wings, and once they were refolded he closed his eyes. He let himself dream—of armadillos, a masked face, fermenting scuppernongs, and other things past.